MEADOWHILL by Annie M Curtis

CHAPTER 1

As we all poured out of the meeting room [obscured] hours I switched my phone back on and noticed [obscured] several incoming messages and a couple of missed calls. I didn't immediately check the messages as Jane and I were in deep conversation about the depressing news we had been given in the meeting.

The company was not doing well and apparently they were to consolidate and were initially asking for voluntary redundancies at all levels with the possibility of more redundancies to follow. I had worked at Dreams head office for over ten years and advanced my way up to the top of a team covering the letting of self catering properties in rural locations. It had it had been a happy time but during the meeting it had fleetingly crossed my mind that perhaps I should take the voluntary redundancy that was being offered and set up my own business.

My phone was in my hand and as it vibrated with an incoming call I automatically answered it without registering the caller surprised when it was Donald my dad's friend and business partner as it was very unusual for him to call me.

"Cathy where have you been I've been trying to get hold of you?" He sounded agitated.

"No what?" I muttered something about a meeting at work but he almost immediately interrupted "The police have been trying to contact you but I guess you've not spoken to them yet so I'm really sorry to be the bearer of bad news Your mum and dad have been involved in a car accident and are both in the hospital."

I stopped in my tracks fear gripping me and my mind going blank for a minute. "How bad is it? Are they hurt badly?" I blurted out.

"I'm sorry but I don't have any more details at this stage except it was an hour or so ago. Your dad had his company ID badge on so the police managed to track me down. I did give them your number but they said your phone was switched off."

I was still stopped in the corridor with Jane next to me "What is it Cathy? What's the matter?" She said as she grabbed hold of my arm she had obviously witnessed my shock.

As I didn't answer she took the phone from me and after a short conversation with Donald grabbed my arm and steered me out of the building and into her car. She sensibly realised I was a bit shaken and drove me straight to our local Accident and Emergency where Donald was waiting for us at the entrance.

"Thank goodness you're here Cathy." He was very pale and looked anxious.

We were immediately taken into a family room by a young nurse then a doctor arrive and proceeded to explain gently that dad had died in the ambulance on the way to hospital after suffering a heart attack at the wheel. Their car had apparently careered straight into the path of an oncoming lorry. He also explained that mum was in theatre but was very badly injured.

I just felt numb as we waited for news and after a long two hour wait the doctor came out to tell us that mum had also died of massive internal injures.

I collapsed onto a chair not able to comprehend how this could have happened. Both my parents dead? It was just too much to take in.

"Oh Cathy I am so very sorry." said Jane who had hardly left my side

After a while a nurse brought us cups of tea and went through the procedure of what would happen next but hardly anything registered and I was grateful that I wasn't on my own. It felt so surreal.

Donald wasn't much better he was sat with his head in his hand and his other arm round me. He had been dad's friend since before I was born and they had started up the business together.

Eventually his wife Angela arrived to take us both home. Jane hugged me tightly and left. "Ill take care of everything at work and ring you in the morning." She looked pale and shaken herself.

The journey to my flat was quiet with Angela and Donald respecting my silence As we pulled up outside they both got out and came inside with me Angela making a cup of tea and pushing a small shot of brandy into my hand. I took the shot she gave me and looked at her "I don't know what to do I cant seem to function."

"It's a terrible shock Cathy and all I need you to do is give me the contact numbers for anybody that needs to know immediately" as I gave her my phone and said "Luke and then Auntie Susan".

Not long after Luke arrived and I went straight into his arms "God Cathy this is awful. What a terrible shock for you."

Auntie Susan and Uncle Derek arrived shortly after and both of them hugged me. I barely spoke but was aware of the murmur of voices as Donald explained what had happened and I could hear Auntie Susan sobbing.

They must have all left at some point but I barely noticed. Luke came to sit by me and put a sandwich with more tea in front of me but I just sat staring blankly at the TV as he kept glancing at me not knowing what to do or say.

"Sorry I cant seem to swallow" I said looking down at the uneaten sandwich. What do I do? What happens now? " I knew I sounded almost hysterical.

"Nothing. You don't have to do anything. Not today anyway." He said reassuringly. "It will take time for it to sink in its just so awful. Come on lets go to bed I'll stay over and be here as long as you need me."

We had been together for a few years but had never moved in together and each had our own places a few miles apart.

The next week or so went by in a blur. People came and went but I couldn't tell you to this day who they were or what they said.

Then on a bleak cold and rainy March day it was the funeral. Auntie Susan and Derek were there with my cousins James and Lizzie, Chrissie my best friend and her husband Rob. Also Donald with his wife Angela and quite a few of the employees from dad's work. Chrissie my best friend and Jane and a couple of my other work colleagues came and of course Luke.

It was a sad day and throughout it all I still felt numb and detached as though I was in a play acting out a part. I didn't cry until the service in the crematorium when Donald gave a short eulogy of what a lovely devoted couple they were but as he spoke and the memories of them and my happy childhood flowed through me the realisation dawned that they had really gone and weren't coming back. Desolation washed over me as I began to realise that my life would never be the same again.

We invited people back to the pub near mum and dad's house afterwards and many people came up and expressed their condolences. Then as people started to say their goodbyes and leave Auntie Susan came and sat down by me hugging me tightly.

"How are you holding up darling."

"I'm really struggling Auntie Susan but I know I need to try to be brave."

She looked concerned and then said gently.

"Give yourself time love. Its going to take a long time to get over this but you will move forward eventually." She was crying herself as she said this.

After a while she said "I think it might be an idea to go to your mum and dad's house Cathy. I popped in last week for the birth certificates but you will need to sort through other stuff. Do you want me to come with you? Do you think you are ready?"

"Yes of course I need to go to the house. In fact I'll go tomorrow but I'll be okay on my own" I had been thinking about the house during the last few days but hadn't plucked up the courage to go knowing it would be just as they had left it. It was where I grew up and held so many memories.

She nodded sympathetically and then I said "I've got an appointment with the Solicitor next week and I was wondering if you could come with me for that."

"Of course I will and if there's anything else we can do you only have to ask." We hugged and she said on a sob "I am going to miss your mum so much." And we hugged harder as I realised she had her own grief to deal losing her only sister.

Luke went back to his flat the day after the funeral as he had a work commitment the following day and I slept surprisingly well, or was it the alcohol I had consumed at the wake. When I woke up the following morning I remembered all that had happened in the last few weeks and then the heaviness returned to my heart. I decided that I had to force myself to get on with life so following a quick cup of tea and a dry biscuit I decided to head off to mum and dad's house, which was a 30 minute drive away.

It was strange as I entered the house I had to stop myself from shouting out a greeting "Its only me". The silence was deafening and at first I wondered round the house picking things up and putting them down remembering my childhood and the happy days spent in this house. Did I want to live here? If I was to stay at Dreams it wouldn't be feasible as it would add valuable travel time to my long days in the heavy North London traffic. It was one of the main reasons I had moved out and got my own place nearer to work.

The house was tidy and clean but I found myself opening cupboards and closing them not having a clue what I was supposed to sort out and ended up sobbing into mum's dressing gown which was hung on the inside of one of the wardrobes. It still smelled of her perfume.

I drifted into my old bedroom memories flooding through me of my childhood and then my teen years. I had taken most of my belongings with me when I moved out and mum had converted the room into a guest room but my old dressing table and wardrobe were still there. This was my safe place, the place I came back to no matter what went on as I grew up. Coming home from school upset that somebody had picked on me or when I didn't do so well with exams. Mum and dad were always there to support and guide me. They were strict but fair and I realised that I had been lucky to have such a carefree happy childhood with such caring parents. My only regret was that I didn't have a brother or sister to share the years with and I found myself selfishly crying as I felt so lonely.

I eventually pulled myself together, cleared the fridge out, collected mum's jewellery and some papers from dads desk drawers then drove home with the vague plan to look through them later.

CHAPTER TWO

After taking the next couple of weeks off I went back to work realising that being at home wasn't actually helping but was adding to the depression. I decided that returning to work and mixing with other people was the way to go although I still felt somewhat numb and detached as if life was carrying on without me and I was tagging along behind.

I was grateful when I saw Jane at the front entrance as I arrived.

"Thought you might need a friend today" she said with a hug and a reassuring smile. Jane and I weren't just work colleagues we were friends as we had worked together for many years. She had recently broken off her engagement and I had been her shoulder to cry on.

My boss also hugged me and said he was glad to see me back. Gradually the day wore on and colleagues stopped asking me if I was okay and I managed to actually concentrate enough to answer my emails that had piled up during my absence.

"Don't worry too much about it Cathy" said my boss "Take your time catching up we're all just glad to see you back and business isn't exactly booming at present."

At lunchtime Jane and I went outside and sat on our usual bench in the nearby park to eat our lunch.

"I know you've got other things on your mind but have you read the emails re the redundancy package. Have you thought what you might do?"

"Yes I did read the emails Jane but to be perfectly honest I haven't a clue at this stage. Have you thought what you might do?"

"Not really" she replied "I don't know whether to hang on in there hoping things buck up or to cut my losses and move on."

It was a strange day and I was glad when it was over. I felt unbelievably tired all of a sudden and as I headed home changed my route and decided to call at Luke's place hoping he could cheer me up. He had been on the periphery the last week or so but he had texted earlier to say that he was working from home that day and wished me luck first day back at work. We had been seeing each other for over three years but hadn't moved in together. It was easy for me to commute to work from my flat and even though he spent the odd night at my place I rarely stayed over at his preferring my independence.

As I opened his front door with the key he had given me I was surprised to hear the sound of soft music playing from upstairs. He had an office in his spare room and I presumed he was working at home with the music as background so I quietly went up not wanting to disturb him but then heard something else - girly giggling and then Luke's voice coming from his bedroom. Thinking nothing of it and that perhaps he was talking to somebody online I gently opened the door. I'm not sure who was more shocked me, Luke or the girl straddling him with blonde curly hair.

"Oh shit" Luke shoved her off and " Cathy I wasn't expecting you".

I simply couldn't speak I recognised the girl immediately as an old college friend. She had always had an eye for Luke but I hadn't seen her in a year or so.

"Well that's blood obvious" I actually felt unbelievably calm again as though this was happening to somebody else and I was just an observer. I just stood there in shock but managed to turn around and clatter back down the stairs out the door and straight into my car with Luke shouting after me.

Drive just drive I said to myself ignoring my ringing phone   I was shaking with shock and anger but I didn't stop until I found myself outside mum and dad's house again half an hour later Without hesitation I rang the doorbell but of course there was no answer. Sobbing I fumbled with the key and let myself in dropping down to sit on the bottom of the stairs and then I cried and cried and cried. Looking back I don't think I was crying about Luke but about my poor parents – I felt so alone and bereft. The grief was overwhelming. How long I sat there I don't know but it was dark and very cold when I finally got up and had to feel for the hall light. I turned the heating on and put the kettle on.   There was no milk and nothing in the fridge but as I sat in front of the TV sipping black coffee I began to feel a little better.

Finally I checked my phone and saw six missed calls from Luke and two from my friend Chrissie.   I rang Chrissie and told her what had happened.

"No that's awful Cathy I wondered why Luke rang asking if you were here but well to be perfectly honest I'm not all that surprised I always felt he had a wandering eye." Chrissie had never really liked Luke and had often said I could do better. "Where are you? Do you want to come over here? Id come to you but I'm babysitting for my sister and have the baby here."

"No I'm fine really Chrissie I think I just need time to think. I'm at mum and dad's house but if you speak to Luke Id rather you didn't tell him."

Next even though my heart was heavy I decided to speak to Luke. He picked up on the first ring.

"Oh God Cathy I'm so sorry" he almost pleaded.

"What you're sorry!! sorry for being found out or are you actually sorry for bonking another woman" There was silence. Then "I really am sorry Cathy You deserve better."

 "Yes I do …..oh go away Luke and leave me alone. I simply cant deal with this now." and I hung up sobbing.

He rang back a few minutes later but I ignored him.

After sitting for another half hour I decided Id better pull myself together. I ordered a takeaway and after searching in kitchen cupboards found an almost empty bottle of gin with some tonic. I poured myself a glass of what was left in the bottle and when the food arrived tucked in. I still felt pretty desolate but the food and gin helped. Eventually I camped out on the sofa and slept I hadn't been able to face sleeping in my old bedroom.

When I woke I was stiff and even though I had only drunk a small amount of gin had a raging headache probably due I decided to the crying. I had a quick shower and dressed back in the same clothes but felt much better. I rang in work and explained that I was running late then headed off back to my own flat for a change of clothes. An hour or so later I was sat at my desk still feeling pretty shitty but desperately trying to look as though I was doing something.

At lunch I headed outside to sit on our usual bench and Jane joined me "Are you okay Cathy I know its been hard but you seem awfully quiet this morning".

I told her about Luke

She was shocked but said " I'm so sorry Cathy not good timing just after your mum and dad passing What a bastard ." She hugged me and we sat mundanely chatting before heading back to the office.

Walking back she hung round my desk for a few minutes "On a separate subject Cathy I know you've got a lot on your mind but don't forget the deadline for the redundancy is next week."

"God I'd completely forgotten My brain is so fuddled at the moment I haven't a clue what I'm going to do".

"Well I've decided to take the redundancy offer and travel abroad. My sister has been begging me to visit her in Rhodes for ages and I would love to see some of the other Greek Islands. What with the bit I've got saved and what they'll pay out for redundancy I should have enough for six months or so while I decide what to do with the rest of my life." She had obviously given it quite a bit of thought.

"That sounds fantastic Jane and I'm sure it's the right thing to do. It sounds very exiting. Um I'll have to give it some serious thought and try to make a sensible decision myself" I said with a heavy heart.

I went back to my flat that night and even though Luke tried to ring I completely ignored him again. I had a restless night tossing and turning going over so many aspects of my life. The decision about work would have to wait I decided because the one person that would have helped me with the decision was my mum and she wasn't here to advise.

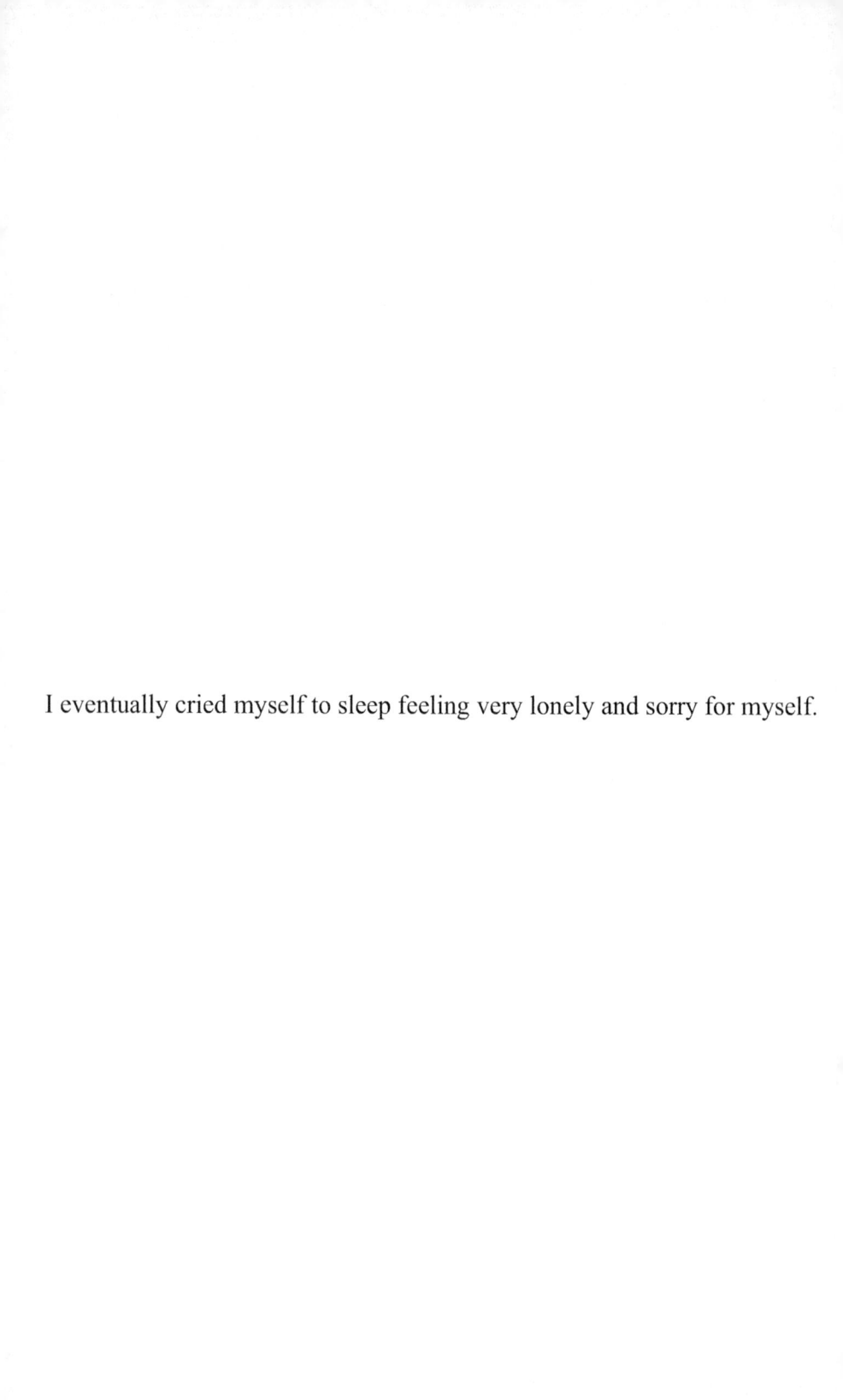

I eventually cried myself to sleep feeling very lonely and sorry for myself.

CHAPTER 3

As promised Auntie Susan came with me to the appointment with the Solicitor, Mr Knowles, a few days later. He was very pleasant and patiently explained everything in great detail. Mum and dad had left wills leaving me the house, some savings in the bank, mum's jewellery and all their belongings. Then there were small insurances on both their lives, which the solicitor said he would follow-up for me.

He paused after relaying all this and then said

"I'm not sure if you are also aware that your dad had recently been left a house in Yorkshire by his brother and also a tidy sum of money."

"I do remember mum and dad saying something about it but they hadn't gone into any detail. I was aware that my dad hadn't spoken to his brother for many years but mum said he had recently died and left part of the family property to my dad." I said trying to cast my mind back to the discussion.

"Well you now inherit the house and the money as well and there's also your dad's share of the business but as regards to that I suggest you go and see Donald Howarth as he'll be able to explain more." It had all suddenly got much more complicated I thought, my head was bursting with it all.

"You are a very well off young lady" said Auntie Susan as we ate lunch later. "What are you going to do? Will you keep the house and stay in it and what about the property your dad was left in Yorkshire?"

"I simply don't know there's so much to think about but I think I might take the redundancy offered at work for a start. I had thought I might like to travel and then maybe set up my own business. I'm so confused and my head's not in the right place but I need to at least make a decision about work while I try and sort out the rest."

"I don't think you should make any decisions while you feel like this but a break with a trip to see this house might help. I remember your mum mentioning about the disagreement your dad had with his brother. It's in a lovely part of the country and I think a change of scenery would do you a lot of good." I had told her about Luke and I knew she was worried about me.

"Perhaps I should go and see this property and decide if I should sell it or not. I've accrued some leave at work and I'm sure under the circumstances I could take some time off. If it's a cottage which I think it probably is then perhaps I could keep it as a holiday home or even let it out as a holiday let." She seemed pleased that it had sparked my curiosity.

"Now I need you to help me look through a few things of mum's as I'm sure some of her better clothes would fit you and there's some pieces of jewellery I would like you to have."

"Don't worry about me darling. I've lost a dear sister and I have so many happy memories of her but I've got Derek and the kids to support me. We'll all be here for you and I'll keep an eye on the house if you want. You must look after yourself Cathy you have the rest of your life to live and they would have wanted you to move forward. We can sort out the clothes and jewellery at a later date. I'm not going anywhere so you can call at any time if you need me."

I went back to my flat feeling a bit chirpier and hopeful for the future. Something to plan for to occupy my mind I thought laughing slightly to myself as there seemed so much to think about. Next day I rang Mr Knowles back and got the details about the house and told him that I would travel up there in a couple of days. He gave me my cousin's number to contact to arrange this and seemed relieved.

Adam Thompson answered his phone straight away "Hello Adam here" and I realised he didn't have my number so wouldn't know who it was. "Oh yes hi this is Cathy Thompson, er …Jonathan's daughter. I'm ringing about the house"

"Oh hello" said the surprised voice on the other end "Can I help you?"

"Well yes I've been to see Mr Knowles the Solicitor today and I was thinking of coming up to see the house if that's okay" There was a short silence as the person on the other end seemed to be digesting this "Umm that shouldn't be a problem. When were you thinking of coming?" he replied.

"I thought the day after tomorrow if that's convenient for you? I've got all the details but I just wondered if you could give me the name of a hotel or B&B not too far away that I could book into"

"No that's not necessary you can stay in the house" came back the reply. "Just let me know when you're on the way and we'll be ready for you."

And that was that.

CHAPTER 4

I had been driving for what seemed forever in fact for over four hours with only a brief stop for the toilet at a motorway services but it now seemed ages since I had left the motorway. My Sat Nav said *arrive in seven minutes* but all I could see were endless fields, stone walls and lots of sheep and cows. Eventually *"you have arrived at your destination"* and as I slowed down I saw two low stone pillars on the left with a sign "Meadowhill".. The car bumped over a cattle grid and then as the road gently sloped uphill I passed through a small copse of trees after which the road widened and there were several buildings huddled together on the left, which looked like a farm. Not sure if I had got it wrong I was just thinking about turning round and going back the way I had come as a woman not much older than me came quickly towards the car with a big smile. I wound down the passenger window.

"Hello are you Cathy?" She seemed pleased to see me "My name is Maggie and we've been expecting you." Two cute little boys had run up excitedly behind her followed by an older woman and a couple of small dogs bounding alongside them.

"Yes I'm Cathy, Cathy Thompson. Are you Adam's wife? Mr Knowles said that Adam my cousin would be here to meet me."

I turned off the engine and was about to get out of the car but before I knew it she was opening the passenger door and getting in shooing the boys and two dogs away at the same time.

"No I'm Ben's wife and I'll take you straight up to the house. Adam is already there."

I was puzzled "Oh this isn't the house then?"

"Ah no she said it's further on – this the farmhouse where we live."

"Oh" I said with surprise as I started up the engine again "Where to now then?"

"Just carry on up the lane and round the bend here to the left. Have you had a good journey you must be shattered?" She didn't wait for a reply "We'll soon have you sorted." We'd driven into another small copse of trees and bushes so I couldn't see much ahead but as I drove slowly round the bend I was shocked when the trees cleared and then I the house.

"Oh my God " I said "This is surely a mistake. This cant be the house I frantically looked around for a cottage then turned to her knowing I was gaping." She laughed "Yes this is Meadowhill House."

There in front of me was a large house not a cottage at all. It was built of the same stone as the farm and other houses I had seen in the area but certainly wasn't a cottage. It was old and quite large set at a right angle with a cobbled courtyard in front. There was ivy growing up at one end and there were daffodils just beginning to flower in the border at the front making it very pretty. The building on the right hand side I realised was a double garage. Whatever I had expected this certainly wasn't it.

"Yes it's a beautiful house just in need of a bit of attention" Maggie said staring at it. "Come on lets get you inside you've come a long way."

Without waiting for a reply she was out of the car, up the two steps and opening the large front door, which didn't appear to be locked. I followed her more slowly still very shell shocked and a bit stiff from my journey.

"Hello Adam you there? She's here." Maggie called out as we stepped over the threshold.

A tall well built man with dark tousled hair appeared from a room at the back of the dark and dowdy hallway. He came towards us smiling "Hi Maggie thought I heard a car – you must be Cathy. Welcome to Meadowhill we've been looking forward to meeting you. Come in Come in." As he ushered me in. He had a rather serious expression and I noted he casually looked me up and down.

He turned and walked towards the back of the house and we followed into a very large, bright, warm kitchen, which was surprisingly modern after the old fashioned dull hallway. He held out his hand and I shook it feeling suddenly shy. "I'm Adam Thompson and this is Maggie my sister-in-law."

"It's very nice to meet you both" I said feeling completely overwhelmed.

He pulled a chair out and ushered me onto it as Maggie put the kettle on and started making a drink "Tea? Coffee?" she said.

"Yes coffee would be very nice please. I'm sorry I'm very confused, surely this isn't the house left to my dad it's not at all what I was expecting."

Maggie and Adam exchanged puzzled glances: "Well yes he said we thought you knew about it. Mr Knowles said it had been explained to you"

"Yes he did but all he told me was that my dad had been left a house on the farm by his brother and I presumed it was a cottage or something, nothing as large as this." I stumbled on feeling stupid.

As Maggie put a mug of coffee and a couple of biscuits in front of me I glanced wildly around. It was a big room with beamed ceilings and double patio doors leading out to a garden.

Maggie sat down next to me but Adam continued standing which unnerved me even more as he was so tall and stern looking.

"Well" said Adam slowly with a drawn out breath " I was going to save this for later but you obviously haven't much idea about the situation so we'll have to fill you in and then if you want Maggie can show you around the house."

"My father David Thompson died just over a year ago as you probably know and left the house to your dad, his brother, Jonathan Thompson. While he left the farm and all the land to me and my two brothers this house was left to your dad and I understand some cash as well. From our point of view this wasn't unexpected as he had told us years ago that he would leave the house to your dad."

"Yes I was very sorry to hear about Uncle David's death." I vaguely remembered mum and dad talking about it at the time and that my dad was very upset. "Was he ill for some time?"

"Yes he was diagnosed with cancer and had treatment but ………" He swallowed and glanced over at Maggie before continuing "I'm not sure if you know but your dad came with your mum to dad's funeral but they were only here the one day and nobody got the chance to discuss the house with him."

He went on "Anyway a few months ago our Solicitor wrote to him informing him about my dad's wishes. He replied that he would like some time to decide what he was going to do. We presumed that he would come and visit but then the next we heard was about the terrible accident. I am so very sorry for your loss losing both your parents at the same time must have been truly awful."

Maggie was nodding by this time and even patted my arm.

"Yes thank you. I have so many questions but to be perfectly honest I haven't a clue what I'm even doing here. Its all been such a shock and then …………other things have happened recently ….." I simply couldn't stop the sob that came out.

He pulled a chair out and sat down then with another deep sigh.

"We thought you might know more than us about the house being left to your dad. I just know that for as long as I can remember he always said that the house was Uncle Jonathan's as half the farm should really have been his anyway"

"As you probably saw when you drove in Meadowhill is a working farm and there is quite a lot of land and several properties. All the family are involved one way or another."

"Yes" I said falteringly "I remember the farm I visited as a little girl and I did know there had been a fall out years ago but I don't know what it was about." There was a silence..

"So do all three of you still live and work on the farm?"

"Yes that's right I'm the eldest then there's Ben and we have a younger brother called Sam. We all still live on the land in various properties but none of us has actually lived in this house for many years. It was just dad the last few years."

Maggie chipped in "Ben and I live in one of the two farm cottages with our two boys then my mum and dad live in the other one, Adam has a barn conversation and Sam has a cottage that he is modernising the other side of the farm for himself and his girlfriend."

"Look Adam I think this is an awful lot for Cathy to take in and she looks shattered how about I introduce her to the house and sort out some food." Maggie was already getting to her feet.

"Yes of course sorry it must be a lot to take in" He got up and looking very intensely at me said slowly as if trying to make me understand "The house is in need of some repair and modernising, mostly cosmetic on the interior but once you've had time to look around I think we should all meet up and have a chat to see what you think. Anyway I'll leave you in Maggie's capable hands" he said tritely and then with a nod at Maggie abruptly strode out of the room.

"Don't mind Adam" said Maggie " He can come across a bit intense when he's got something on his mind."

"Come on lets show you whats what. The kitchen as you can see was modernised a couple of years ago and through that door she said pointing to where Adam had disappeared is a utility room and the back door." She opened the fridge "I've put some basics in. Would you like something to eat now?"

"No thank you I said I'll have something later." I was actually starving but far to embarrassed to admit it and the biscuits had slightly taken the edge off. She was very kind but I couldn't let her wait on me.

We walked back through into the hallway which really was very dark and dull compared to the kitchen and then into another room on the right.

"This room is the living room and where David spent the last year or so of his life as he sadly wasn't able to get up the stairs".

It was a big room with a large stone fireplace but was very cluttered with lots of furniture. There was a bed the other side of the fireplace and beyond the bed there was a well worn chair placed directly in front of patio doors at the back, which looked out over the garden and farmland.

"As I say David lived in here the last year and spent a lot of time looking out of the window watching the comings and goings. He was still very involved in the running of the farm right to the end." She said with a little hitch in her voice and I could tell how much she had cared for her father-in-law.

She saw me looking and glanced away then turned back laughing and I realised how pretty she was. "He was a difficult old sod but I still miss him."

"Anyway lets move on it's a bit depressing in here." Back across the hall we went to a door facing which led into a smaller room with a beautiful ornate wooden desk and some very dusty bookshelves heaving with books of all shapes and sizes.. There was another smaller fireplace, which looked original.

Back out into the hall Maggie turned right into another doorway. This room had obviously been a dining room at some point but the large table was completely covered in dust sheets and allsorts of bits and bobs piled up on it. "Sorry its not been used for so long everything gets dumped in here I just wish that I had time to go through it and sort it all out."

I must have been so quiet that she looked at me a bit concerned and said "You okay do you want to keep looking. That's more or less it down here but there is the upstairs. You must be exhausted."

"I'm not so bad and of course yes please I'm intrigued and a bit overwhelmed."

"Lets show you something a bit more positive" said Maggie as she turned right at the top of the stairs into a lovely bedroom. It was large and airy and had obviously been decorated in the not too distant past. There was a double bed with clean modern blue and white flowered bedding and freshly painted walls and blue curtains.

"We did this room up for David while he was in hospital but he never actually used it as he simply wasn't up for the challenge of the stairs when he came home. Mum and me came in when we knew you were coming and spruced it up with fresh bedding etc. We thought you could use it during your stay".

"Its lovely I said and looks very comfortable. Thank you so much." Maggie opened a door off and there was a modern en-suite shower room, which looked unused, and as if it had been modernised quite recently.

"Well at least you have somewhere comfortable to sleep while you are here. The other option would have been for you to stay in the pub in the village but it seemed silly when this is here and saves you travelling backwards and forwards. Especially when legally the house is yours now."

There were three other bedrooms of various sizes and a large very old fashioned bathroom plus a couple of what seemed to be store cupboards.

The house had a nice feel to it but in my whirring brain all I could think about was that I would have to sell it as there was no way I could do all this work myself. I was beginning to feel quite panicky. What the hell had I done coming here to a place and people I didn't know.

As I stood thinking we heard voices below and Maggie went to the top of the stairs. Below was Adam and another man who actually looked incredibly like him but a bit shorter and bulkier.. He had a ruddier complexion like the look of somebody who spent a lot of time outdoors. I must have looked confused as Maggie said "Oh let me introduce you to my husband Ben and yes they are very alike."

"Nice to meet you Cathy" said Ben with a booming voice. "If you can unlock your car we'll bring your luggage in. I'm not sure you will be comfortable in here but I'm afraid we're full up at the cottage and seeing as how the house IS yours that you would want your own space rather than being in the village."

"Oh my keys are in the kitchen" I said as we walked back downstairs.

"What do you think of the place so far?" said Adam obviously curious as to what I thought.

"Well …………..I think it's a gorgeous old house but much too large for me I'm afraid and in need of so much work I couldn't possibly take it on"

I stopped at a loss as to what else to say and saw Adam and Ben exchange worried looks and I wondered what they had expected.

 "Perhaps once Cathy's settled in and rested we should all sit down and have a chat" said Adam pleasantly "Maybe tomorrow evening here? You can meet the rest of the family at the same time." It wasn't so much an invitation as a statement."

Adam brought my small case and bag in and carried them upstairs..

"Will you be okay here on your own?" said Maggie "We are only minutes away if you need anything".

"Yes that's fine I'm used to living on my own just not in such a big house" this came out in a nervous laugh.

Adam showed me the keys for the front and back doors and explained that the house was quite secure I exchanged mobile numbers with both him and Maggie who also gave me the landline number for her at the farm.

"Ring me if there's anything at all" said Maggie as she left with a reassuring smile and off they went.

As they all left I locked the front door behind them and wondered back into the kitchen sitting down at the large table staring around. *What the hell I thought.*

I opened the fridge and was grateful to find it well stocked. I found a pizza and popped it into the microwave as the Aga looked far to complicated to even consider. There were also a couple of bottles of wine so I poured myself a glass of red and ate a couple of slices of pizza before taking the rest and another glass of wine up to the bedroom with me.

This is strange I thought as I changed into pyjamas and unpacked my toiletries. I texted Chrissie and Auntie Susan and told them I had arrived safely but was very tired and would speak to them in the morning. I ignored several missed calls and texts from Luke.

Settling down in my new surroundings it took me a while to get to sleep what with the strange bed and strange house and the quiet. I got up twice once to check the bedroom door was locked and picked up my phone to make sure there was a signal. There was also a landline at the side of the bed with a dialling tone and eventually I dozed off totally exhausted.

CHAPTER 5

I woke early to the sound of birds singing and a cock crowing. I lay there for a while not quite sure where I was then the familiar heavy dread descended on me as I realised what had happened in the last few weeks. I missed my mum and dad so much and also reluctantly admitted to myself that I missed the familiarity of Luke as well.

Then the sun started to peep though the curtains and I pulled myself together determined to greet the new day and new experiences.

After showering I dressed in clean jeans and a t-shirt and went down to the kitchen where I found some bread and made toast and a cup of instant coffee. I wandered round looking again in each room realising it really would make a lovely family house. It just needed somebody with a lot of cash and spare time to bring it back to life but I couldn't see that being me.

From the front upstairs window I found the view of the surrounding countryside was mostly obscured by trees and shrubbery just coming to life in the early Spring sunshine. It was all so green and lush I thought and a world away from the busy roads of North London. Looking out through one of the back bedroom windows there was a garden immediately below then beyond that a field sloping down towards some trees and I could just see the glint of water beyond. Perhaps there was a river or stream I thought deciding to explore later.

Picking up my hoodie I ventured into the utility room to the back door and realised with a shock that it had been unlocked all night. That was the problem with living in a flat I thought there was no back door to worry about.

Immediately outside the back door there was a sort of cottage garden that I had seen from the window above and it was obvious that somebody looked after it as there were little rows of what looked like vegetables and herbs planted just beginning to push their way up through the soil.. There was a brick wall on the right with a door that I guessed led into the garages I had seen at the front of the house. Ten at the very bottom was an archway through which I could see another building.

There was a small lawned area off to the other side of the house edged by mature trees and bushes then fields. I walked down to the end of the garden to the field beyond along a rough path and into the trees through which I could definitely see water.

It was so beautiful I thought and stood contemplating for a few minutes as I looked around. All I could see for miles was countryside with gently rolling hills. I could hear the low rumble of what I thought could be a tractor off in the distance but apart from that it was very peaceful with just the slight swish of tree branches and birds singing.

I moved on and tentatively followed the path curious as to what the water beyond was. After a few minutes the trees cleared and I was rewarded by the sight of a large expanse of tranquil water. It was so picturesque it took my breath away and I realised it was a small lake.

I sat down on a mound of dry glass and breathing deeply drank in the lovely sight feeling more relaxed than I had for a long time.

Five minutes or so passed must have passed and then….

"Hello. Are you exploring?" a deep voice behind me said.

I nearly jumped out of my skin he had come up behind me so quietly and I turned to see Adam smiling at me.

"Yes I thought I would take a look around. It's a beautiful property and this, well this view is gorgeous" I replied.

"Pretty impressive isn't it?" He said proudly. "The lake actually belongs to Meadowhill."

"What? This is yours? You've got to be kidding me its breathtaking and I had no idea the property was so large":

"Yes there are the buildings, the farmland and the lake. Its been in the family for a several generations. Did you not know about it …… us at all?"

"Not really. He was a man of few words my dad. Of course I knew Uncle David lived on a farm up here and I do vaguely remember visiting when I was little but I don't recollect the lake. To be perfectly honest my dad never talked about his past much." I said feeling quite guilty that I hadn't discussed my dad's early life with him before it was too late.

"Yes well I understand they fell out after granddad's death 20 odd years ago so I suppose you wouldn't have visited since then. I understand that your dad didn't want to work on the farm but wanted to move away and start up his own business."

There was a quiet pause both of us just staring out at the lake

"If you'd like one of us could take you out in a boat if you'd like, although it probably be down to me as Ben doesn't get much spare time off from the farm and Sam's not always around. Its not very large but I've always found it good to view the surrounding shore from a boat and get the lay of the land so to speak."

"Don't you work on the farm? " I was embarrassed as the invitation took me by surprise.

"Yeah sometimes but I'm a Vet and have my own business. I have a practice the other side of the village."

"You're a vet?" I said with surprise and slight embarrassment that I had presumed all the boys were farmers.

"Yes er ….. like your dad I didn't want to go into the family business in the farming sense and I managed to persuade dad to let me study to be a vet instead. Maybe my dad had learned a hard lesson from what happened with your dad so he decided to go with it and encouraged me."

"I went to Agricultural College then off to University which took quite a few years but I came back every chance I got and helped out around the farm. After finally qualifying I came back and joined the local Vet's practice then when he retired I took over the practice. It works quite well as I can still be involved in the running of the farm and looking after the livestock. Adam works on the farm when he has time but he's also a chartered surveyor and is renovating his own house." This was the most information he had imparted since I arrived and I began to relax a little.

"What about your mum? If I remember she died when you were all quite young. Hope you don't mind my asking."

"Mum died when I was 7, Ben was 5 and Adam was only 3. I remember her but it's a bit blurry. She died very suddenly of a brain haemorrhage and I don't think dad ever got over it."

"How sad" I muttered "I'm so sorry" and couldn't think of anything else to say.

He didn't reply and there was that awkward silence between us again.

"Yes I think it would be nice to go out on the lake if you have the time but not sure when." I ventured, rushing on to cover the awkwardness "I didn't really expect to be here for more than a couple of nights. It's all been a bit much to take in and there is so much to think about. Perhaps I should stay for a few days. Its so peaceful here away from the bustle of my normal life" This was more to myself than him and he didn't reply. He seemed to be lost in thought gazing out over the water.

"Is there fish in the lake?" I had no idea about fish or farm animals or lakes or anything but was uncomfortable with the silence so blundered on.

"Yes but I wont bore you with all that. When I was younger I did a bit of fishing here, we all did but its just Sam who fishes now. You'll meet him later as he's coming up to the house to meet you "

"Anyway I'm really sorry but I'll have to he off I've got calls to do. I just wanted to make sure you had settled in okay." All of a sudden he switched and was more business like.. " Make yourself at home and if there's anything you need please call one of us. You might want to walk down to the farm and see Maggie I'm sure she'd love to introduce you to the terrible twins. I'll see you later around seven at the house if that's okay with you?"

"Yes that's fine. See you later"

I got a fleeting smile as he left.

I decided to go back to the house and make a few calls feeling that I the needed to catch up with the world – my world.

Firstly I rang Chrissie back and re-assured her that I was absolutely fine and although still feeling very down that I had made the right decision to come and look at the house as it had given me something other than myself to think about.

Secondly I rang Auntie Susan and caught up with her, following which I rang Donald.

"Hello Cathy how are you coping? I understand you've gone off to see the property you've inherited. How's that working out? Will you be selling it?"

"Oh hello Donald I hope you're coping too. I'm not too bad thank you and yes I will be selling. Its just a bit more complicated than I had expected as its quite a large property in need of some work".

"Well when you get back I wonder if you could come down to the office. Along with everything else you've inherited the stake in the business and I need to go over a few things with you. I want you to give some thought as to how much you want to be involved in the company. There are also things I cannot move forward on without your signature as things stand at present."

"Oh dear I'd never given the business much thought Donald. Sorry if this has caused complications for you and you must be missing dad yourself" I felt a sense of dread at having something else I needed to make a decision about.

"Yes we're all missing Jonathan very much, he's left a large gap in our everyday lives. Perhaps some time next week you could come here and then back to our house to have a meal with myself and Angela and tell us all about your house in Yorkshire. We care about you Cathy and I also owe it to your dad to make sure you are okay." He and Angela were my also my godparents.

"Oh Donald that's so lovely and yes to both. I'll give you another call in a day or so and let you know when I'll be back."

Lastly I decided to ring Luke. For this I went to sit outside at the back of the house on a wooden bench where I thought I might feel calmer.

He didn't immediately pick up but then on the second try . "Hi Cathy I've been worried sick. Where are you and are you okay? "

"I'm fine Luke but I need you to stop ringing me please."

"Don't be like that Cathy. I've told you I care about you." He said more angrily this time.

"Care? It didn't look like it when you had that blonde bimbo bouncing about in your bed!!! And by the way how long had that been going on?"

There was a long pause and then "I know I've made a huge mistake Cathy but I just want a chance to put it right. I just want things back the way they were." He ignored my question, which made me wonder if it had been much more than a one time fling and that made me even more determined.

"No Luke you know what I've decided that I don't want to go back to the way things were. Yes it was a huge mistake and I don't think I'll ever forgive you but we were going nowhere and I think we both knew it. When I have sorted things out here I fully intend to go travelling for a while on my own."

"Cathy no please. I could come with you I've got some money put by we could travel together. Take time to sort out our relationship."

"No Luke there is no relationship to sort out. Its finished please don't keep ringing me." And I hung up on a sob.

Strangely I didn't feel that sad. I hadn't known that I was going to make that decision before I called him but somehow I felt relieved. Luke and I were over and I needed to move forward.

After sitting contemplating things for a while and having a bit of a cry I decided I needed to pull myself together. Mum and dad wouldn't want me to sit around moping.

Deciding to take Adam's advice I locked up the house being careful to include the back door and walked down the lane to the farm As I rounded the bend I could see the farm just ahead of me. I hadn't really paid much attention when I had arrived the day before but now I could there were two lovely semi-detached cottages with a cobbled area in front and a large barn type building to the side then on the other side a large yard with chickens running about, a couple of goats and some farm machinery.

As I got to the cottage gate the older woman I had seen with Maggie greeted me

"Hello you must be Cathy? I'm Carole, Maggie's mum. Would you like to come in for a cup of tea and meet the rest of the family?"

She was an older version of Maggie with a lovely homely face. "I'm pleased to meet you and yes I'm Cathy and yes I would like to meet them " I laughed.

She led the way into the first cottage and a lovely sight greeted my eyes. A large modern kitchen with a centre isle and Maggie was obviously baking with the help of the two boys.

Maggie's face lit up when she saw me "Oh you'll have to excuse the mess Cathy. We're all covered in flour. Say hello to Cathy boys. Come in and mum can you put the kettle on. Tea, coffee, scone?" She was wiping her hands on her jeans as she spoke.

She explained that the boys were seven year old identical twins a fact which she didn't need to tell me as they were like two peas in a pod. They muttered hello and grinned shyly at me before she ushered them out of the back door. "Look there's granddad go and see if he needs any help and take the dogs with you." As she shooed them and two young dogs out through the back door.

Maggie quickly put the tray in the Aga and at the same time was pulling a chair out and dusting it over with a tea towel. "Please sit down its so lovely you decided to walk down. I was hoping you would. Its nice to have some female company." She glanced guiltily at her mum "well nearer my own age anyway." Her mother laughed and rolled her eyes as she was busy with the kettle and mugs.

We all sat down companionably at the floury kitchen table a large mug of tea was put down in front of me and a warm scone. I immediately felt at home as though this was what I did every day. So over the tea and scones I asked about the cottage garden.

"Oh that's mum's project and she wont need much encouragement to tell you all about it" as Carole commenced to explain that yes it was such a convenient sheltered spot and over the past few years she had had quite a lot of success with a variety of vegetables, herbs and some fruits. "Most of which we eat ourselves but some of the fruits I make into jam and chutneys and have started to sell locally. Its taken a few years to get to grips with it but I really enjoy it. Maggie here is too busy with the children and helps out around the farm with the chickens and milking etc. so its my own little project."

They asked me about my mum and dad and consoled me about my loss and the accident. I avoided mentioning Luke. I wasn't ready to explain to strangers.

After a while we went outside the back door and I was introduced to Paul who was Maggie's dad. The two boys were helping to spread some clean straw for the goats although they had more in their hair than there was on the floor. I was introduced to the goats were called Gertie and Joan and were a recent addition apparently.

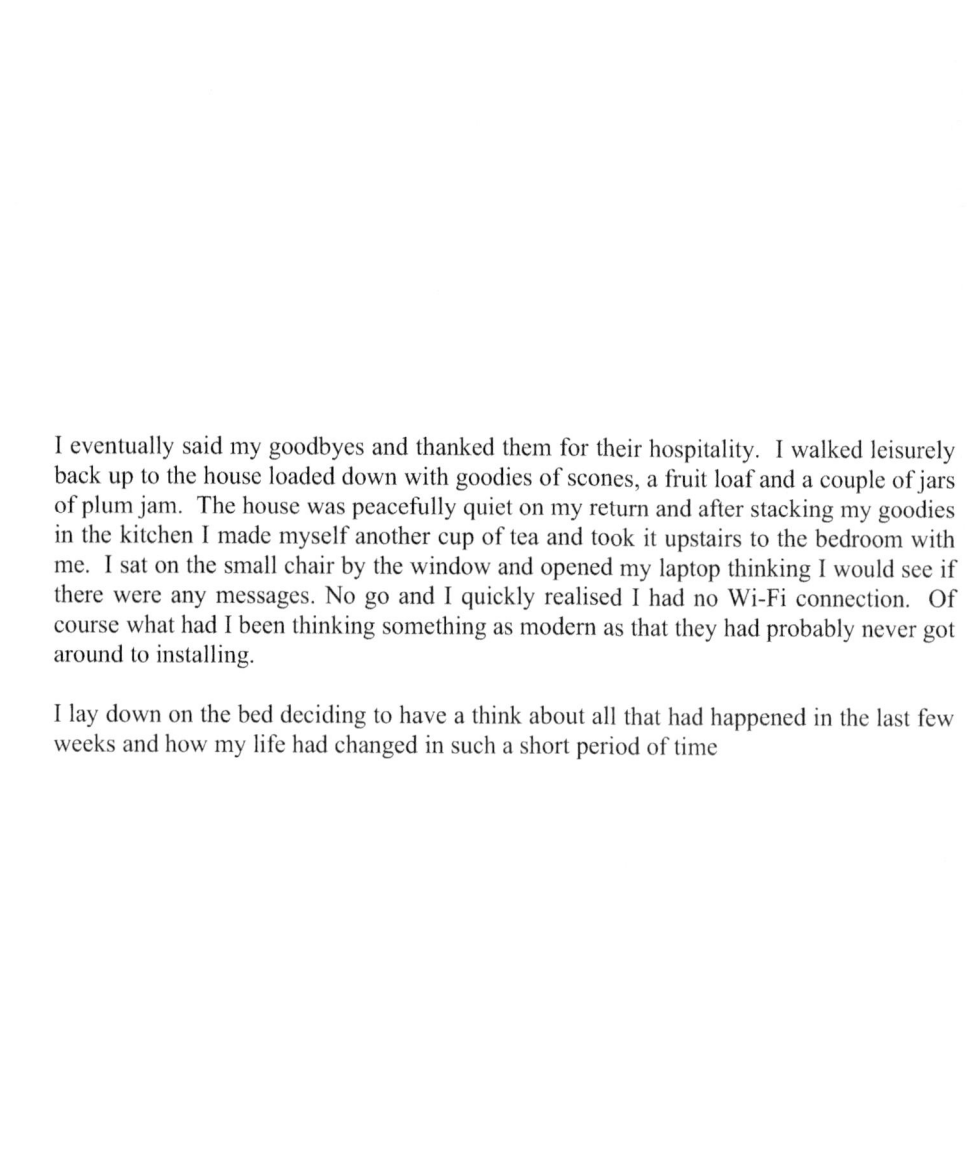

I eventually said my goodbyes and thanked them for their hospitality. I walked leisurely back up to the house loaded down with goodies of scones, a fruit loaf and a couple of jars of plum jam. The house was peacefully quiet on my return and after stacking my goodies in the kitchen I made myself another cup of tea and took it upstairs to the bedroom with me. I sat on the small chair by the window and opened my laptop thinking I would see if there were any messages. No go and I quickly realised I had no Wi-Fi connection. Of course what had I been thinking something as modern as that they had probably never got around to installing.

I lay down on the bed deciding to have a think about all that had happened in the last few weeks and how my life had changed in such a short period of time

CHAPTER 6

I must have dozed off as some time later I woke to find the sun going down and the smell of something delicious cooking. After splashing my face with water and cleaning my teeth, I ran a comb through by hair and dashed a sliver of lipstick on before going down to investigate.

I found Adam in the kitchen with Maggie. "Oh I came up and you were napping so I left you to it. You must be exhausted with all that's happened to you recently" she smiled kindly.

Adam didn't even look round he was working at the stove and just checking on a large dish, which was in the oven. There was a beautiful golden Labrador stretched out on the floor near the table and I bent down to stroke it "Oh and this is Lady" said Maggie "She's Adam's dog but the two dogs down at the farm were her puppies. We've got two sheepdogs at the farm as well. Do you like dogs?"

"Yes" I said but I've never had one of my own We had one at home when I was younger" I said remembering Trixie our golden retriever.

"Lasagne okay? You're not vegetarian or anything are you?" said Adam interrupting my thoughts.

"Oh yes please and no I'm not. I'm sorry I must have dozed off" I said "and I should have thought with you all coming that you might want something to eat."

"Its no problem" he said with a flash of that lovely smile "We often all eat together" he explained pleasantly "Sometimes its easier for us to catch up this way as life is so busy around here." Maggie was preparing a salad.

"Sit down and lets have a glass of wine" he said grabbing some glasses from a cupboard. "White? Red?"

"I'll have a small glass of white please. I feel terrible you've supplied all this food and made me feel so welcome I really do owe you at least to have helped in the kitchen."

"This house is yours and we are using it as though its still ours so the least we can do is make you comfortable and anyway we are family – cousins in fact" said Maggie.

"Oh about that er......I should explain" I started to say but just then another man walked into the kitchen.

"Sam you're here already come and meet Cathy." cried Maggie. Sam was obviously a few years younger than Ben and Adam taller and lankier and even more good looking.

He rather awkwardly went to hug me then changed his mind and shook my hand obviously not sure of the status here.

"Welcome, I understand we're related? I didn't even know about you until last week but then again they don't tell me much" He said affably.

Again I started to speak "Yes it's all been a bit of a shock really and………. well it's lovely to meet you too."

"You having wine Sam? "offered Adam.

"No I wont Adam I'm driving. What's cooking I'm starving" as he wondered over to the cooker and bent down to look in.

I decided to leave the explanations for now as just at that moment Ben also arrived with his father-in-law Paul.

"We've left the boys with Carole for an hour or so." said Ben "Bath time and bed."

We all sat down around the large kitchen table and Adam served up the lasagne and salad with slices of garlic bread. I realised that I hadn't actually eaten a proper meal for a few days and tucked in enthusiastically.

As we were coming to the end and Sam was helping himself to seconds Adam gave a small nervous cough and said "I think we need to talk to you Cathy about the house. Are you absolutely set on selling?"

"Yes I think I'll have to" I said "Sadly I don't see that I have much choice. It's a long way from where I'm living and lovely as the farm and grounds are the house needs a quite a bit of work before I could make it a holiday home and its far too large for me to live in on my own. I wanted to use some of the money I have inherited to travel if possible as my life has   changed so much in the last month or so" I knew I was babbling but was embarrassed as they were all looking at me expectantly.

"I thought you had a boyfriend" said Maggie "Wouldn't he be interested in getting involved with the house and move up here with you?.".

"No no" I stuttered even more embarrassed "He's, he's   well no he wouldn't be involved".

There was a silence and I dared a glance around the table "Wouldn't you want to have the house for yourselves? It would make a lovely family home especially for you Ben and Maggie - perhaps we could come to some arrangement re the purchase"

It was Ben this time who answered "We haven't really got the capital to release to buy it outright and do it up but perhaps now we need to re-think about that side of it more seriously if you really intend to sell." he said looking at Adam with a furrowed brow.

"The one thing we all agree on is that we don't want it to be sold to somebody outside of the family as that would mean them having access to the farm and land. It would be difficult to retain our privacy. Also we wouldn't be in control of what they did with it. It's a dilemma that's worried us for some time but we were waiting for you to come on board as legally it belongs to you." This was Adam and said almost angrily. What is his problem I thought.

"There's also the question of the cottage garden" said Maggie quietly frowning at Adam. "My mum and dad have put an awful lot of work into it and truth be told it doesn't belong to us as its on your property so if you sell it we would lose it". She looked at me a bit apologetically.

"Oh but it's beautiful and I certainly feel that I don't have any right to object. This is your family home" I said I was beginning to feel a bit panicky that they obviously had been waiting for me to come and help them with decisions. I wasn't in any position to help anybody else make decisions when I couldn't make any myself.

"I am so sorry things are a lot more complicated than I had anticipated and unfortunately I'm not in the right place myself at the moment to make decisions. To be honest I'm pretty overwhelmed by the whole thing"

"There is no rush with this" Maggie said quietly.

"Why don't you take some time to think things over. Perhaps if you get to know the house a little better you might feel different." this was a bit more kindly from Ben. Adam didn't say anything more but looked grumpy and worried.

"I have to say I've enjoyed being here so far and you have all been so kind. If you really don't mind I think I might stay for a few more days. Its so peaceful here and I don't have to rush back for a week or so."

They all seemed pretty relieved by this and relaxed into general chatter about the farm while starting to clear up the remains of the meal.

"By the way Adam I meant to ask where is the nearest Wi-Fi connection is as I hadn't thought of course you don't have such modern facilities here at the farm. There are a few things back home that I need to attend to."

"For God's sake we don't live in the dark ages" snapped Adam angrily "We do have Wi-Fi you just need the code to connect. I suppose I should have thought about it before" he added more quietly.

There was an awkward silence so I meekly said "Thank you" with a polite smile "That would help enormously. Sorry I didn't mean ,,,,,"

"We had it put in a couple of years ago" said Sam winking at me "Need to keep up with the modern times even up here you know"

As we finished off clearing the kitchen Maggie and Ben left with Paul. "Try to relax and enjoy your time here" said Maggie "When all said and done it is your family home too. Don't you worry about Adam he doesn't mean anything by it." Oh doesn't he I thought. He obviously thought I was a complete idiot with no understanding of their way of life. He wasn't wrong.

Shortly after Adam left with Sam in tow and I watched them companionably walk down the path to the archway the dog following faithfully behind. I was still none the wiser as to who lived in the house beyond the archway but I suspected it was Adam himself.

Later that night in my bed I struggled to sleep badly regretting the nap I'd had earlier so I got up and sat down again in the chair by the window and set up my laptop logging on with the code Adam had given me. This time I managed to access my emails. There was a lovely chatty one from Jane telling me that she had now accepted the redundancy package from work and was busy planning her trip to see her sister in Greece who apparently had a small hotel and letting business on the island of Rhodes.

I went back to my bed a little bit depressed I wasn't sure what I was going to do – travel on my own? Perhaps Jane would let me tag along? I knew that I needed to contact the office by Monday with a decision if I was going to take the redundancy package and as today was Saturday that only left one day but I thought I knew what my decision was going to be.

Perhaps I could re-locate up here and do up the house while living in it and setting up my own business at the same time but it seemed such a huge undertaking I didn't think I was capable of that plus at the end of the day why would I want to live alone in such a large house and even though they were my family (in a way) I didn't know them very well. Adam seem quite hostile to me at times for some unfathomable reason.

Eventually I fell into a troubled sleep.

CHAPTER 7

Next morning I was still awake early even though I had been up so late. I had a shower and after a leisurely breakfast of boiled egg and toast I wandered outside to take another look around the walled garden. Just beyond the wall to the side of the garages there were what I thought could be some fruit trees although I didn't know what type. I saw Paul walking up the path with a basket and guessed he was coming to pluck some veg or herbs but as he didn't appear to have seen me I made a hasty retreat back into the house not feeling up to further conversation about my plans this morning.

I fired up my laptop again and emailed my boss asking if I could put in for the voluntary redundancy. I had come to a decision in the early hours to take the redundancy as financially there was no need for me to stay at Dreams. It made sense and it felt good to have at least made one decision. He would get my email in the morning so hopefully get back to me fairly quickly then I could move forward with other decisions. Perhaps I should next give some thought to letting my flat go and move back into mum and dad's house. I had moved out to be nearer work and have my own independence but it didn't make sense to have two places to live and if I was finishing at Dreams I wouldn't have that lengthy commute every day.

Then I rang Auntie Susan and had a lovely chat telling her all about the house and that I had decided to stay a few more days. I could tell that she was relieved to hear from me and said that I sounded more positive about the future. We chatted generally about her family and ended the call with me promising to keep in touch and visit her when I got home.

I decided to explore the house again in more detail because if I was to make a decision about its future then I should see just how much work it would take to make it liveable.

The first room I looked into was the living room and I tried to look beyond the clutter. It was a big room with a large picture window at the front looking out onto the front drive and at the back French doors giving a lovely view of the garden and farmland beyond. The big feature stone fireplace was beautiful and I felt that if the room was stripped back it could be made into a lovely spacious living room.

Next was the small room at the front and in actual fact I decided that it wouldn't take much to make this a small comfortable space perhaps as a home office. The hallway was a big job as the floor tiles, which looked original, would need repairing and cleaning and of course it would need completely redecorating as would the whole house.

I sat down when I got into the dining room and started to idly look through some of the boxes. There was a pile of old vinyl records that looked fascinating and I looked round to see if there was something to play them on and I found an old dusty turntable under one of the sheets. Lifting the lid I plugged it into the wall and took a Beatles record out of its cover, gave it a wipe with the dustsheet and gingerly placed it on the turntable. I could just about remember how this worked from years before at my mum's house. As the boys sprang into song with Please, Please Me I jigged around the room exploring more boxes coming across a stack of old photographs.

"Hmm hmm" a loud cough came from the doorway. "Enjoying yourself I see" it was Sam with a big smile on his face. "Oh sorry!" I said guiltily "Maybe I shouldn't have been going through this stuff. It probably all belongs to the family."

I quickly took the arm of the turntable. "No its fantastic" said Sam "Lovely to hear those sounds after so long and you're right we should go through this stuff and sort it out. We could have a party and play all the old vinyl. What fun that would be."

I realised he wasn't alone as a girl edged shyly into the room. "This is Katie my girlfriend" said Sam. "Meet Cathy" he said nudging her gently forward. Katie was a very pretty slim girl with long blonde hair probably in her early twenties. I said "Hi nice to meet you." She seemed fascinated with the records obviously not having seen vinyl before. "OMG I've heard of so many of these groups" she said flicking through them.. "Such a weird way of playing music can we hear some more?" Sam and I glanced at each other mutually amused by her obvious delight.

After another 10 minutes or so of us chatting and looking at the records Sam said "Well we'll be off Cathy sorry to interrupt you. I really must try to get out of the practice of just dropping in here as if it were home but I wanted Katie to meet you. This house is yours now and you need your privacy. We'll wait to see what you decide about its future."

"No stop! Wait! Please stay for a cup of tea or coffee with me I'm so curious to find out more about your own plans with your house etc." I genuinely was interested.

"Yes that would be lovely" said Katie eagerly "I love spending time in this house it has such a vibe."

"Ah that's what it is a vibe" I laughed "but I know just what you mean".

Over coffee and biscuits Sam told me a bit about his plans "When I've finished renovating my house Katie is going to move in. I'm doing it for both of us to share."

"I'm an artist you see" explained Katie "and Sam's going to build me a studio. I mostly sketch and have managed to sell quite a few" she said excitedly. "And….. " carried on Sam "As I help out on the farm its best if I'm based here but I was also looking at setting up some fishing parties on the lake to bring in more revenue." They were both so enthusiastic about their future plans it wasn't hard to be happy for them.

As they were leaving a short time later I reassured Sam that they were welcome to drop in anytime they wanted. "Thank you Cathy and I hope you decide to stay." They both gave me a hug before they happily trotted off down the lane towards the farm.

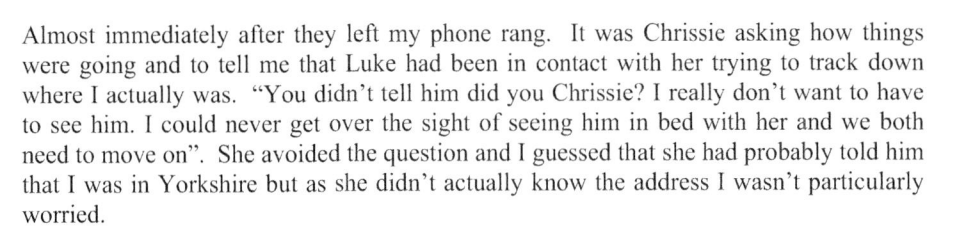

Almost immediately after they left my phone rang. It was Chrissie asking how things were going and to tell me that Luke had been in contact with her trying to track down where I actually was. "You didn't tell him did you Chrissie? I really don't want to have to see him. I could never get over the sight of seeing him in bed with her and we both need to move on". She avoided the question and I guessed that she had probably told him that I was in Yorkshire but as she didn't actually know the address I wasn't particularly worried.

"Actually Cathy that's not all as I have news of my own" I could tell she was desperate to tell me something. "You're pregnant" I said immediately. "How did you know?" she laughed surprised. "I don't know we've been friends for so long perhaps it was a sixth sense but I am so very very happy for you Chrissie and for Rob. I know its what you've wanted for a long time."

We chatted some more about her pregnancy and when she was due and how she was feeling. After our call finished I felt much more cheerful as I really was very happy for her and looked forward to sharing the happy event.

I drifted back into the kitchen and made myself some pasta then decided to have a shower and go to bed early.

CHAPTER 8

The following morning was Monday and so after a quick coffee I decided that I needed to get away from the house for a while so grabbed a bag and drove down towards where I thought the village would be. Not having seen anything remotely resembling a village when I arrived I guessed it was further on down the main road. If I was to stay for a few extra days then I would need to see if I could buy some clothes. I had originally thought that I would only be staying two nights so had only brought a change of clothes.

So I turned left out of the farm gate passing another gated lane about 200 yards further down the road on the left guessing that must be another entrance into the farm property. Then after another five minutes more buildings started to appear mostly in similar stone to the farm and house. Parking up at the side of a pub called the Farmers Arms (of course it was) I wandered down what appeared to be the main street. It was quiet as it was still early but I was surprised to find there were quite a few shops and I could see another pub further down the street. Many of the shops were not open yet but the butchers, bakers and a small supermarket were already getting quite busy.. A bit further down the street I found a lovely little boutique-type clothes shop which disappointingly was closed with a sign on the door stating it would be open in an hour.

Walking back towards the car I noticed a coffee shop open on the opposite side of the road so went in ordering a pastry and a coffee from a young girl who looked enquiringly at me. I went and sat outside on the pavement where a couple of tables and chairs had been laid out and hadn't been there more than five minutes when I jumped as a car beeped and pulled up at the curb at the side of me. Maggie leaned over "Hi there are you okay? Exploring? I'm just dropping these two off at school. Do you want to hop in and come with us then I could give you a lift back?"

"If you don't mind I wont this time" I leaned into the car smiling over at the boys "I'm on a mission to do a bit of shopping as I've not brought enough clothes" I explained.

"Okay Tricia will be open over the road soon and you should be able to get something there. She has some quite nice stuff. Perhaps see you later". she replied as she and both the boys waved at me cheerfully. The young girl was wiping one of the other tables "Aaah she said you're up at Meadowhill. I wondered where you had popped up from as we don't really get many sightseers this early in the day."

"Do you get many tourists then?" She seemed pleasant and happy to chat.

"Oh yes we get quite a few but most either stay at the pub down the road or there's a little B&B just outside the village and they tend to breakfast there so we don't get them until a bit later. It was my idea to put the tables and chairs out on good days to get the attention of passing trade. Of course we are weather dependent and I get a bit bored when its not busy but hopefully as the weather's looking good today it might get busier later on. The area is very popular with walkers all year round."

She bustled off inside the shop and I sat watching the passing traffic for a while then when she came back out I thanked her and strolled back to the boutique.

Maggie was right there was some nice stuff Tricia was very helpful and friendly. I bought a couple of t-shirts, a shirt and a pair of chinos deciding that for now that would help and making a mental note that they didn't sell underwear so I would need to do a bit of washing back at the house. On the way back to the car the smell from the bakery lured me in and I bought a freshly baked loaf and then I crossed back over the road into another shop selling outdoor wear and bought a pair of walking shoes plus some wellies and walking shoes...

When I got back the house was quiet and peaceful. There was obviously nobody around so I went into the utility to grapple with the workings of the washer and put my underwear and t-shirts in. I heard angry voices drifting through the back door and popped my head out. Through the archway I could see Adam talking to a blonde woman. She didn't look too happy and was pointing her finger aggressively into his chest and shouting into his face. They were obviously arguing but he replied something quietly and she turned on her heel and walked away. A couple of seconds later I heard a car rev up and drive off down the lane. Adam glanced my way obviously aware I was watching and I guiltily withdrew back into the house not wanting him to think I was nosey.

An hour later after I had made myself a sandwich in the kitchen with the lovely fresh bread I fired up my laptop again to find that my redundancy request had been accepted. My boss had messaged back that he was very sorry to lose me but understood completely mentioning that I would need to go back in to the office for a couple of weeks while all the paperwork was being drawn up and work my notice. I replied that I would be back the following Monday and would check in with him then. That gave me four or five days to spend at Meadowhill so in effect four or five days to make a decision about the house.

There was a polite knock on the open back door. "Hello Cathy are you there?" To my surprise it was Adam "I have a couple of hours free and wondered if you wanted to take a trip on the lake?" He seemed quite amiable today after his grumpiness the last time I had seen him.

"Oh yes that would be lovely just let me change my shoes and get a jacket".

"We can go in the car" said Adam as we left the house by the back door.

"Oh not down through the garden then?" I said surprised.

He grinned "No we have a small boat moored up a little way along where there is a small jetty."

I followed him down the garden and through the arch where there was a jeep parked on a small gravel driveway. I couldn't help my curiosity as I could now see the building I had only glimpsed from the garden. "Is this where you live?"

"Yes it's a barn conversion. Sam and I converted it with the help of some local building lads. Come on lady you can come as well." He opened the door for me to get in and the back of the jeep for the dog to climb in.

He drove down the lane past the farm buildings and then turned right up a track at the side of the large barn. "That's the lambing barn next to the cottages and just beyond it the hay barn". I could see two or three vehicles parked up on the ground to the side and also behind I could see more outbuildings. We drove through a couple of fields and the track went slightly downhill. At the bottom there was a small jetty with a little motorboat moored up and also a rowing boat.

"Which do you prefer me rowing or the motorboat? If you are up to it and trust me the rowing boat might be more leisurely". In the end we went in the rowing boat.

It was very pleasant sitting back and gliding along smoothly on the water. Lady was very obedient and sat in the middle and I gently stroked her head and ears as we moved along. Adam was an expert rower and it was quite a pleasurable sight to see him flexing his muscles. I realised that if things had been different I might find him very attractive. He seemed competent and happy on the water. It wasn't a big lake and as he manoeuvred round he talked me through various sights on the shore. You could just about make out the house through the trees and he showed me where Sam was renovating his house just further along from the farm.

"So………….have you had any thoughts about our conversations the other night about what you might do regarding the house?"

So, I thought, that's why he's brought me out to get me on my own to talk about the house and my plans.

"Well no but I have decided to take redundancy from my job and it was just accepted this morning. I love my job but the company isn't doing too well and rather than hang on in there I decided the time was right to bail out as financially I'm now in a position to do so."

"What will you do next?" he said in surprise "Move here into the house?" I could sense a bit of the anxiety coming back into his voice now.

"Well I thought I might travel but to where I don't know. My friend is off to Rhodes where her sister owns a property and I think she is going to use it as a base while exploring the Greek Islands. It has occurred to me that I should go with her but I cant seem to make decisions easily at the moment."

"What about the boyfriend? Is he definitely out of the picture?"

"Er yes that's definitely finished." I paused then carried on "I found him in bed with another girl a couple of weeks after my mum and dad died." I self-consciously pretended to watch a bird dipping down to the water.

"Oh no that's not good" he said with raised eyebrows. "What a bastard you must be devastated. Was it serious?" He said this on a much softer note and seemed genuinely sorry for me.

"Well I thought so at one time but to be perfectly honest I think we were just drifting." I said as nonchalantly as I could.

He nodded "Yes I know what that's like." Which made me wonder about the girl I had witnessed him obviously arguing with earlier in the day.

There was a pause then "I hope you realise we don't want to put pressure on you. Take your time it sounds as if you've had a lot of trauma in your life recently but please keep us in mind if you do decide to sell. It affects us all so much."

"I promise as soon as I decide I will let you know I said. I think I'm probably going to go back to my flat on Saturday and will try to make a decision before then."

"As I said there's no rush it's a huge decision why not wait and come back in a few weeks and then make a decision"

He smiled reassuringly and seemed so genuine that I felt something shift in our relationship. We had decided that we liked and understood each other a little better.

"Okay back to shore." He said and a few minutes later we pulled up at the jetty. His phone pinged and as he glanced at it he said "Sorry duty calls can I drop you back at the house?"

"No please drop me at the farm I'd like to explore a bit more and see what goes on there if that's okay with you. Not that its really got anything to do with me but Id like to show an interest at least."

"Yep of course."

He dropped me at the front of the cottages and I knocked on the front door.

"Maggie's not in" said Carole as she popped her head out of her own front door. "She dropped the boys after school and has gone off to the supermarket for some grocery shopping. Would you like a cuppa?"

"That would be lovely Carole" and I stepped into her house. It was very similar in layout to Ben and Maggie's house and we walked straight through to the back kitchen. The boys were playing with Lego at a large kitchen table and I sat down next to one, not being sure which was which. "Can I join in?" I said

"Yes please we're building a castle" said the nearest twin glancing up. I mouthed to Carole "Which is which?" She laughed and immediately introduced us "This little man is Joseph and this one is James. We tell them apart by their freckles don't we?" Both boys giggled at this. "Say hi to Cathy boys and help her to know which of you is which."
"Oh no" said James very seriously "She's new we cant give away secrets yet." Both Carole and I laughed heartily. "Well I obviously have a way to go to get to know you yet but I'll try I said. Perhaps if I help you build the castle that would be a start." They both nodded vigorously and giggling again.

I spent a lovely hour or so helping with the Lego and chatting to Carole mostly about the kitchen garden. She obviously loved tending to it. "I haven't actually seen you up there" I said "No I come very early in the morning and I'm quiet as I am aware its your property now and would hate to disturb you."

"You wont be disturbing me at all and anyway I'm going back home on Friday or Saturday so you'll have it all back to yourself." She put her hand on mine and said "I hope you can find it in yourself to stay Cathy. You are a lovely girl and a pleasure to be around."

Just then Maggie arrived back with bags of shopping. "Here you are mum this is your stuff I hope I've remembered everything. Hi Cathy Hi boys Looks like Cathy has been playing nice with you." She handed them both a carton of orange and a packet of crisps and sent them outside to play.

"I'm glad I bumped into you Cathy I'm going out tomorrow night down in the village with some girlfriends and I wondered if you'd like to join us?"

"That would be lovely thanks for asking me" I said rather flattered that she had asked "I've was thinking of having a bit of a look around the farm if you feel like showing me. I've just been down to the lake and though it might be nice to see a bit more".

"You've been down to the lake?" she said surprised "Yes Adam took me in a row boat" "Oh" she looked even more surprised.

"Tell you what I've got to put all this shopping away before milking but lets find dad and let him take you round. He knows every nook and cranny and is more knowledgeable than me." She glanced at her watch

We found Paul in the first building at the back of the house which was the milking parlour. "Hello" he said "I'm just moving one of the milking machines that's a bit old now and we are going to use the space for the two new goats. Come and have a look we've found them a home down at the end. One of the farm lads helped me construct it yesterday." It was lovely a little arched building at the end with new straw spread out The two goats nosily wondered over to see who I was.

"Are you familiar with farm animals" asked Paul. "No I haven't a clue" I laughed "I've not been on a farm since visiting here when I was a very young girl"

"Out beyond here you can see we have a small herd of cows and further afield we have 30 or so sheep." He said gazing out of the barn.

"Come and see the pigs We are quite new to pig farming as they've not been kept on the farm for many years. We have only have 6 so far, one male and five sows." As we moved out of the barn into the yard.

"Oh the smell" I said covering my nose with my hand "but aren't they gorgeous"

"Yes but you cant get too attached as several will eventually go for slaughter." "Oh no" I said "Cant you keep them I've heard they make lovely pets" "Yes I suppose you could" he said laughing at me. "You'll have to come by in a month to see the litters. That's when they are really cute."

"Such a lot to take care of" I said quite bowled over by how many animals there were.

"Yes it's a time consuming job keeping it all clean and tidy" said Paul "and come milking time it can get pretty hectic with all available hands on deck. Then there's lambing season around the corner which keeps everybody busy."

"Where are Ben and the farm hands now" I said curious to know who did what on the farm. "Well Ben and a lad called Derek are out checking walls and fences at the moment Its non-stop and as they need to keep a look out for gaps where foxes can get in as they play havoc with the livestock. Plus they'll be checking the sheep especially the ones about to lamb. We need to keep a close eye on them."

"Well I'm exhausted just thinking about it all. Thank you very much for showing me around Paul its all very interesting. I'm going to head off back to the house if you don't mind."

"Do you want a lift up to the house? I think Maggie.........."

"Oh no thanks the walk will do me good." I felt as though I had taken up too much of his time so said my goodbyes and strolled up to the house. It had clouded over and started to rain on the way back up the lane and I hurried to get indoors.

Back in the house I walked upstairs looking into each of the bedrooms which were all just very dusty and in need of decorating. Two of them were still furnished with old fashioned beds and wardrobes but obviously hadn't been used for many years. It wouldn't take too much to smarten these up I thought but then stopped myself as I realised that it would take years before I could even consider spending that much time and money on them and why would I want to.

After checking on my washing and hanging it on an airer I found in a corner in the utility room I made myself something to eat and then settled down in the chair in my room with my laptop catching up on news and Facebook.

CHAPTER 9

Next morning I decided to follow-up on Adam's invitation and walked down through the arch to his house but was disappointed to find that his jeep wasn't there and he was obviously out working. From this angle I could see that the shingle drive continued down from his house to the gate directly onto the main road which confirmed what I had noticed when I drove into the village. There were two other old buildings on the right backing onto the garages of the main house which appeared empty and just shells of long past storage or cattle sheds.

I also looked into the two garages which were surprisingly cleaned out. I had half expected to find an old car or farm machinery in there but apart from a few old crates in one corner they were completely empty.

My phone rang and it was Maggie asking if I would like to eat with them later and then Ben would run us down into the village to meet with her friends. I accepted gratefully feeling I needed girlie company and arranged times with her.

So at 6.30 I wondered down to the farm and was met with a flustered looking Maggie

"I hope chicken casserole will be alright but I'm sorry I'm running a bit late"

"What can I do to help?" I said hanging my coat on the hook behind the door.

"No …. well you could just get plates and cutlery out for me if you really don't mind. Not much of a hostess am I getting you to muck in. There'll be five of us."

"Honestly Maggie I really don't mind." I said opening drawers and cupboards with her pointing me in the right direction.

Finally she called the boys in from where they were playing outside and the four of us sat down to eat.

"Is Ben not joining us?" I said wondering where he was. "Yes hopefully he'll be here in a minute." just as he appeared at the back door looking dirty and tired. "Sorry love I'll just wash up and be with you".

When he joined us he explained that they had lost a couple of cows on the way to the milking parlour as they had wondered off up the lane and it had taken him a while to get them sorted. He entertained the boys with actions of him shooing them down the lane with a stick.

"It can be long hours on the farm Cathy and things don't always go to plan. Neither of us gets out much to socialise but I knew that Maggie wanted to go tonight and take you with her. Get up the stairs love and get your glad rags on." This was directed to Maggie with an affectionate tap on her backside as she walked towards the door.

"Be 20 minutes Cathy" she said laughing.

Ben and I cleared the table and then he also disappeared upstairs with the boys to put them to bed. I loaded the dishes into the dishwasher and was nearly done when Maggie came back down. "Oh Cathy you should have left it for Ben later. Come on before anything else develops we'll just knock on for dad as he said he would drive us down".

Maggie was transformed looking very pretty in jeans and a frilly blouse with some make-up on "Oh we scrub up well when we have to" she laughed when I complimented her.

Paul dropped us outside the Farmers Arms and we were met inside by Tricia from the clothes shop and another girl who was introduced as Sheila. "Sorry we're a bit late girls you know how it is."

We got a couple of bottles of wine and four glasses from the bar and found a table in the window.

"Cheers" said Sheila and we all touched glasses. "Now tell us all about your glamorous city life Cathy. Do you go to loads of swish parties and out to shows and things?"

"No not really" I said laughing. "Its definitely not glamorous. I work 8 until 4 or 5.30 sometimes 6 but the commuting takes up hours as the roads are really busy. It grinds you down sometimes. You have no idea how lovely and tranquil it is up here."

"Well I wouldn't call it that hey girls" said Sheila wryly "It gets really busy in summer with lots of tourists and the roads around town can get really congested and lets not go there with the parking situation. Then if you live on a farm like Maggie here you work extremely long hours just to make a decent living."

"And we have to travel distances just for a big supermarket shop" added Tricia "which is not good sometimes with the bad weather we can get in the winter months."

"Yes I never thought about all that" I said thoughtfully "Life is very different but everything seems at a much slower more relaxed pace".

"That's because you are not working here" said Sheila not unkindly "You are on holiday are you not?"

"I suppose wherever you live has its advantages and disadvantages" I said a bit defensively. Why did I get the impression these girls thought I was so different from them coming from the *big city* as they called it.

To make conversation I asked Sheila what she did for her job. "Oh I work in the estate agents" she said "So I suppose fairly normal office hours. Perhaps if you decide to sell the house at Meadowhill you could give us the business." It was more of an observation than a question and I glanced at Maggie but she was looking across the room at a couple who had just come into the pub. She suddenly jumped up with a smile on her face throwing her arms around the lady who had come in.

"Oh here's mum and dad" said Tricia as she blew a kiss across to them.

Maggie and the lady hugged warmly obviously pleased to see each other and then she turned and beckoned me over.

"Cathy please come and meet Janet and Frank, Tricia's parents" as I reached her and she drew me towards them.

"Janet this is David's niece Cathy."

Janet gave me a wonderful smile and I could see she was curious. "Well I'm very pleased to meet you Cathy."

As her husband headed over to the bar she came and sat down at our table giving a hug to Tricia as she did so "Janet was housekeeper and cook up at the house for a many years" explained Maggie.

"I worked at the house from the boys being young, generally looking after the house and cooking an evening meal for them. David had his hands full what with the farm and three young boys to care for after Grace died." explained Janet

"Oh yes Adam told me about his mum passing away when they were young, so very sad" I suddenly realised I had been so caught up with my own problems that I hadn't thought much about their family life growing up without a mum.

She then said very quietly "I knew your dad as well, we all went to school together."

"Really" I said with surprise "I had no idea...... " but then I saw her face light up as Adam came towards us. As she got up he caught her in a big bear hug "Not seen you for ages Janet. How are you and the old man?"

"Yes we're good love he's over there come and have a catch up – sorry" she looked at me apologetically as they both moved away over to the bar where I saw Adam grasp her husband's hand and shake it vigorously. I also noticed he wasn't alone the woman I had seen him having an argument with the day or so before was one step behind and I saw Janet step towards her and they briefly spoke.

Maggie returned to sit beside me "Sorry perhaps we should have mentioned Janet to you. She's almost part of the family as is Tricia".

"I'd love to chat with her more" I said "She said that she knew my dad. I would love to hear about when he was younger and living up here".

"She doesn't come up to the house much nowadays I think it makes her sad but I'll ask her to tea some time if you're around much longer" replied Maggie thoughtfully. Tricia nodded in agreement.

The night moved on as a couple more of Maggie's friends joined us and more wine was ordered. It was quite noisy and I began to feel a little light headed. Janet and her husband waved over as they left and I noticed that Adam and his girlfriend had sat down in a corner talking quite intently. Neither of them looked particularly happy and a short time later she got up and exited through the back door where the toilets were and Adam wandered over to the bar hitching onto a stool chatting with the landlord and a group of men.

Some time later Sheila and I went to the ladies and as we exited she stopped and nudged me to look at the back door where Adam's girlfriend was stood leaning against another man just outside. They were very close "Look at that cow Stella she's always been the same never satisfied with the gorgeous Adam" says Sheila "Lets not mention it to Maggie it'll only upset her".

As we sat back down I saw her whisper into Tricia's ear and as they both turned Stella walked back into the pub. She spoke to Adam who barely acknowledged her and carried on chatting to the barman. She then came over to Maggie and said "I'm off Maggie. See you around and generally nodded at everyone at the table".

When she'd gone Tricia leaned forward to Maggie and said "I don't care that you've got history with her I simply cant stand her and I hate the way she just picks Adam up and drops him when she feels like it. He's too easy going with her."

"I'm not so sure its quite like that" said Maggie defensively glancing over at Adam "I think they both use each other. I also think that he feels if people think they are a couple he doesn't have to bother with anybody else."

By this time I realised that we were all getting quite drunk and a couple of the girls had decided to go home.

As Sheila left with Tricia she gave me a hug and said "Lovely to meet you and would be great to see you again if you up here but guess its pretty boring compared to what you are used to down South."

"No its not Sheila believe me I've had a lovely evening and everybody is so friendly and kind." I reassured her as she left.

"Hey you two ladies need a lift home" this was from Adam "Its okay I've not had a drink but it looks as though somebody has had a few as Maggie stumbled towards him".

"Oh yes Adam that would be lovely please" she definitely looked a bit worse for wear and I felt a bit wobbly myself.

Adam pulled up at the cottage and got out to take Maggie to the door waiting until she was safely inside before coming back for me.

As we pulled up at the house he again got out and came to walk me to the door.

"I'm fine really Adam" I said as to my dismay I swayed towards him.

He caught me with both hands on my shoulders laughing "I think the lady does protest too much. Here let me." As he took the key from me and opened the door all the while propping me up with one arm.

As we stepped inside I took the key from him and said "Thank you very much kind Sir I think I'll be okay from here" again swaying towards him.

He steadied me again and said "Are you sure you can get upstairs to bed? Or do you need help?"

There was a definite twinkle in his eye and we were so close I felt his breath on my face and a tingle of excitement spread down my spine but then I realised he was laughing at me.

"No I'm fine I can manage" I said indignantly half pushing him towards the door.

"Okay well make sure you lock up and I'll see you tomorrow. Ring if you need anything." as he walked backwards through the door.

I had to hold onto the door while I locked it and then stumbled into the kitchen to check the back door. As I made it up to my bedroom my phone rang and it was Adam.

"Are you okay? I think I should have stayed to see you up to bed" He actually sounded quite concerned this time.

"Yes all locked up and safe" I giggled and hung up as I fell back onto the bed.

I woke feeling slightly sick and with the most horrendous headache. When I looked at my phone it was 9.30 and there were two missed calls from Maggie and one from Adam. I immediately texted both of them to say that I had only just woken up with a hangover but that I was okay.

Over a coffee and two Paracetamol in the kitchen I thought back to the night before. I really had enjoyed myself but remembering my drunken state at the end of the night hoped I hadn't shown myself up and felt slightly embarrassed. I realised that Adam was a very attractive man and because I hadn't had any male company for some time and was very drunk that I had imagined something between us.

An hour or so later I rang Maggie to check how she was feeling.

"I had the most awful headache when I woke but mum and dad came to the rescue helping to get the kids off to school." She said laughing. "How are you feeling?"

"I'm okay but wanted to let you know that I had a good time. Everybody was really nice and kind. Thank you for asking me." I replied.

"I enjoyed it too" she said "But I definitely wont be drinking as much next time. Ben was okay with me but it meant he had more to do this morning as I wasn't at my best. Have you decided when you'll head off home?"

"I thought I might go on Thursday to avoid the weekend traffic but if its okay with everybody I've decided to come back in a couple of weeks once I've finished work." I said thoughtfully.

"Well I for one don't mind and I'm sure the boys wouldn't either." She said happily.

Chapter 10

The journey back home on Thursday was terrible as it rained almost all the way and visibility on the motorway was difficult. It took all my concentration and over five hours so that when I finally reached the flat I was exhausted. Even though it was only early evening after texting Auntie Susan that I had got home safe I crawled into bed feeling depressed and cold. The flat didn't seem as welcoming as I had expected.

The following day I contacted an estate agent and put the flat on the market having decided that I would definitely move into mum and dad's house. Over the weekend I started to clear out the flat making several journeys again feeling relieved that I had managed to make yet another decision.

I called in at Auntie Susan's and spent a couple of hours catching up with the family before going back to mum and dad's and sleeping in my old bedroom for the first time in many years. This felt more like home I decided.

On Sunday I went to see Donald where over a lovely meal we discussed the business and it was agreed that I would become a *sleeping partner*. I had no interest in the running of the business and told Donald that he knew what he was doing so I would leave him to it. We were both happy with the arrangement and Donald said he would sort out the legalities later in the week with the Solicitor. I left feeling relieved that yet another decision had been crossed off my list.

On Monday I returned to work and realised that I had made the right decision about the redundancy. Business was very slow and within a day or so I had caught up with my work. Jane was due to leave for Greece the following week and several other members of staff were also leaving so a goodbye party was arranged for the Saturday at a local wine bar.

"Where are you up to with your plans for the future?" Jane asked on our last lunchtime before she finished.

"I am disgusted with myself that I haven't made any plans" I said feeling a bit of a failure.

"I think you are being very hard on yourself Cathy. You have taken redundancy, put your flat on the market and become a sleeping partner in your dad's firm. Those are tremendous steps to have taken and I don't think you should be beating yourself up. Its only been a short while since your mum and dad died." She said giving me a hug.

"Do you want to come with me to Greece for the summer at least? You would be very welcome and we could have sun and fun" she said laughing.

I laughed with her but said "No Jane I'm going to go back to the house in Yorkshire and make a decision about it before I move on. Believe it or not I've missed being there this week and hate to admit it but feel like there is something drawing me back."

"Could he be called Adam? Or Sam even?" she said with a raised eyebrow's and a knowing look.

"No no, you've got it wrong Jane. Its nothing like that for goodness sake"

I instantly replied needing to explain the situation to her. "They both have girlfriends and Sam's way to young for me anyway."

"Um well I'm not so sure Cathy. I haven't met them but it sounds to me like there's some sparks there in particular with Adam and talking about sparks look whose just walked in". She said her eyes looking alarmed.

I swivelled round on my high stool at the bar to see Luke and a couple of his mates just coming through the door.

"Well you know what Jane I might sneak out and go home. I really don't want …." But it was too late.

Luke was in front of me smiling. "Well fancy meeting you here. How are you? I didn't know you were back. You might have let me know."

"Oh hi Luke" I forced a smile and nodded at his mates behind him then said very quietly "We are not together so I didn't need to tell you I was back and anyway its only for a short time. I have er… plans."

"I saw your flat was up for sale - where are you staying back at your parent's? I think we should get together and talk things through and anyway I've got some of your things at my place. How about we get together tomorrow night and I could let you have them."

"No I don't think so and I haven't missed my things so just throw them out. Anyway Luke I was just off so ……." and I got up to move.

"Don't be like that Cathy". His eyes were pleading but I hardened myself and replied coolly. "Enjoy your night boys, see ya" and both Jane and I left quickly jumping into a cab right outside the door.

"Come back to mine" said Jane glancing at my face aware that I was a bit upset "We can open a bottle of wine and put loud music on. I move out tomorrow so don't think my neighbours could complain much."

"Okay I think I will, especially as you're setting out on your adventures tomorrow and I wont see you for a while." Bumping into Luke had upset me more than I wanted to admit.

We talked well into the night discussing Jane's exciting plans. She was all packed and was flying to Rhodes the following afternoon. "I am so happy for you Jane after all that happened with your ex. You go girl and have a fantastic time and meet a gorgeous Greek God."

"I have to admit I really am excited, sun, sea, sand and ……….whatever life throws my way." She said laughing then on a more serious note "You know Cathy I've been thinking about this house and your family up in Yorkshire. Why cant you do the house up and rent it out. It sounds as though it would make a very good air B&B for groups looking for self-catering country retreat. You don't have to move up there as you could manage it from down here or you could move into it yourself and run a business from there."

"I've thought about all this Jane over and over. I couldn't let the house out as it is on family land and whoever stayed in it would have to access it through their property. It would be really mean of me to do that and although I love the house its too big for me to live in on my own. No I think I'm going to sell it back to the family at a reduced price. It'll be a battle to convince them but I cant see any other way.

"Would they want to buy it and can they financially afford it?" She asked.

"Well its already been mentioned so I'm not sure but I'm going to put it to them when I get back and see what we can work out between us. Really it's the only sensible solution."

"It sounds as it you have become quite close especially to Maggie, would you still visit if you sold it to them?"

"I'm not sure if they would want me to" I said sadly "The only reason I have been welcomed really is because my dad was left the house, so if I sold it I wouldn't really have any reason to visit".

"Well you'll have to let me know how it all goes but I've got a strange feeling about the situation Cathy that they might not let you go quite so easily."

This made me laugh "You're just an old romantic Jane. Its really not like that at all."

We said our goodbyes shortly after and I got a taxi back to the house. I was so sad to see her go as we had become quite close over the last few years but I was happy for her and wished her all the best on her travels with a promise to keep in touch.

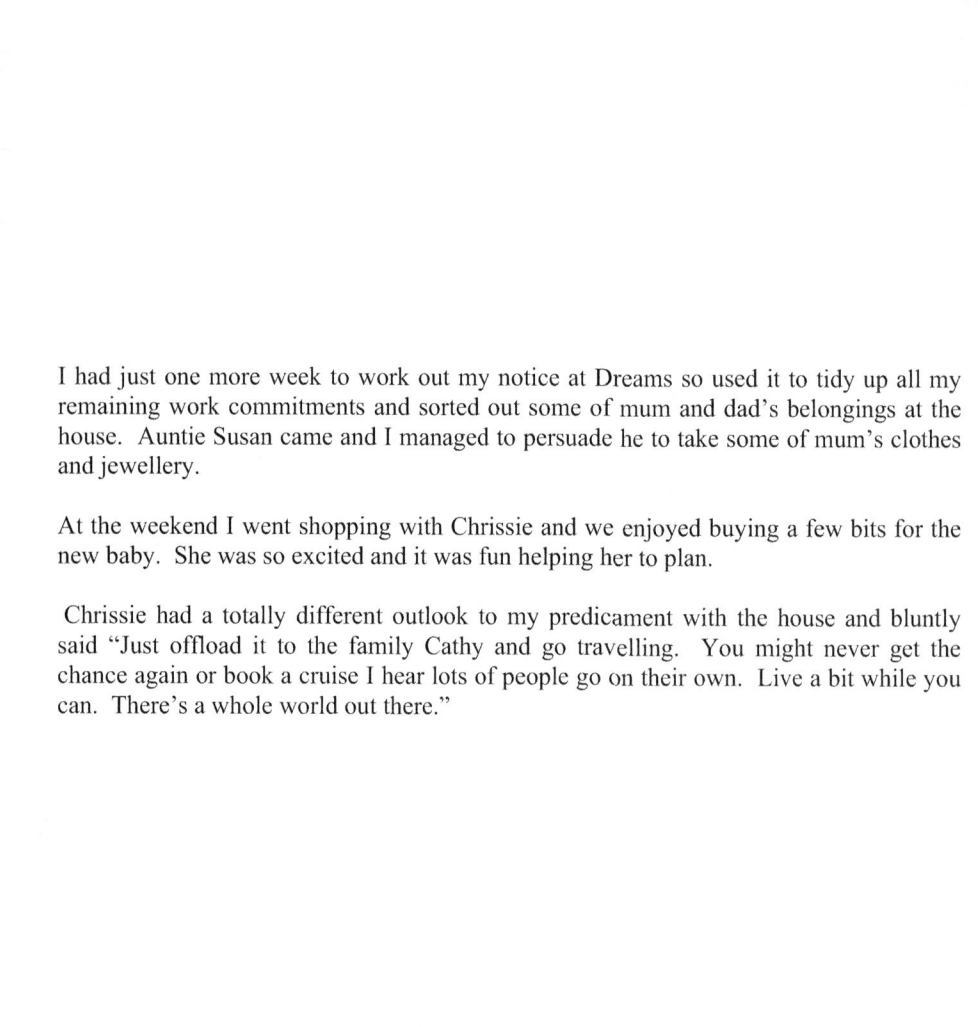

I had just one more week to work out my notice at Dreams so used it to tidy up all my remaining work commitments and sorted out some of mum and dad's belongings at the house. Auntie Susan came and I managed to persuade he to take some of mum's clothes and jewellery.

At the weekend I went shopping with Chrissie and we enjoyed buying a few bits for the new baby. She was so excited and it was fun helping her to plan.

Chrissie had a totally different outlook to my predicament with the house and bluntly said "Just offload it to the family Cathy and go travelling. You might never get the chance again or book a cruise I hear lots of people go on their own. Live a bit while you can. There's a whole world out there."

CHAPTER 11

The following Monday I had set off later in the day than planned as I was busy clearing out the flat as the estate agent had informed me that there were several people keen to view it. It was dark by the time I turned into the farm lane and rattled over the now familiar cattle grid.

I had spoken to Maggie on the phone who had told me that they had been very busy on the farm as it was lambing season but that she would pop into the house and put a few essentials in the fridge.

"Please don't go to any fuss Maggie I can bring some groceries with me."

It seemed very quiet as I drove up past the cottages with just a few lights on but as I rounded the bend the car lights lit up for a minute on a courting couple at the side of the barn. I was surprised and couldn't make them out at first but then I realised that it was Maggie and Adam. What no it couldn't be!! I was so shocked that I almost swerved off the track but managed to continue driving coming to an abrupt stop outside the house. Grabbing a couple of bags I unlocked the front door and headed for the kitchen immediately starting to throw things into the fridge and cupboards. I was swearing out loud to myself as I just couldn't believe what I had just seen and felt slightly sick.

I should have known it was all too good to be true I thought. I had been so looking forward to coming back to the people I was beginning to consider as family but I obviously had completely misjudged them.

Shortly after Adam came through the back door looking a bit red in the face and slightly dishevelled. "I saw the lights go on. We weren't expecting you so late."

"Well that's obvious" I said angrily turning to face him determined to speak my mind when the door burst open again and Maggie fell in looking equally dishevelled with Ben closely following behind.

"I saw you pass and I've brought you a steak pie mum made earlier" she said as she wildly held out a foil covered dish. She cast a guilty look over at Ben and then said "Sorry Cathy if you saw us er …." She was bright red by this time and looked frantically at Ben.

"Its just that we don't get much privacy in our busy house and ………." she muttered and then it was Adam that spoke. " For God's sake what have you two been up to?" with raised eyebrows and a confused look.

"Ben, it was Ben of course it was" I blurted out and then as three sets of eyes turned to me I continued "I was just so shocked as it looked like……..Adam" I faltered feebly as all three of them burst out laughing. Maggie looked relieved. "Adam you thought it was Adam??" More hilarious laughter

"Oh God sorry" I said feeling mortified.

I could have sank into the floor but Maggie came over and gave me a hug "Welcome back to the mad Thompson family its so lovely to have you here again" she said still looking embarrassed but laughing.

"Is there enough pie for all of us" said Ben seemingly quite unperturbed peering under the cover "I'm starving."

"Well that's probably because of your outdoor sexual exploits brother dear" said Adam mischievously as Ben mock punched him on the shoulder.

Maggie put the steak pie in the oven and added some oven chips while I cut some bread and Adam poured wine then we all sat around the table chatting.

"We were in the lambing barn until late as one of the ewes was having trouble delivering on her own" Maggie had eventually managed to compose herself enough to look at her brother-in-law "but with Adam's help we got there in the end. I think it was the relief and…….. "

"Where were you?" said Adam obviously enjoying the situation enormously "No don't tell me its better if I don't know."

"Well it'll be a while before I get the vision out of my head" I said laughing then feeling bad as Maggie started to go red again.

"Actually its funnier than you think" said Adam obviously still highly amused "Because many years ago Maggie and I went on a double date with Ben and Stella but by the second date we had swapped and the rest is history. He gave Ben an amused look and his sister-in-law an affectionate peck on the cheek."

"Err umm I should tell you that Stella and I are finally finished for good" he said more seriously almost as an afterthought. "Its drifted on for far too long and she's gone back with that Mike that she was seeing when I was away at Uni."

"Well I'm glad you've finally come to your senses Adam. You deserve so much better." Said Maggie with Ben nodding agreement. "Its been on, then off, then on again for years."

I was enjoying their banter and thought to myself this feels so right sat here as part of a family. Then a voice quietly whispered in my ear "So you thought me and Maggie eh??" and I turned to look him in the face and saw his eyes sparkling with amusement.

He then quickly turned away and poured us all a second glass of wine as I took a deep breath and said.

"I've been thinking about the house while I was at home and I think you should buy it from me. We could come to some arrangement about the price." I hadn't meant to say it so bluntly but the look Adam had given me had unnerved me and my mouth had opened before I had time to formulate what and when I was going to say it.

There was deadly silence then Maggie said "Well that's that then. I think we were all hoping that you might take it on and stay here but I suppose realistically that's not going to happen."

"Okay let's get everybody together in a day or so and have a proper discussion about finances" this very quickly from Adam with a resigned serious face.

"I'm sorry but I've thought and thought about it and I think it's the most sensible solution. This is your home not mine and I almost feel like just giving it back to you. I feel like I'm stealing from you."

"Don't be ridiculous." said Ben "The house was left to your dad for a reason and we need to respect dad's wishes. I'm sure that its within our reach to raise the money between us but like Adam says we'll have a meeting about it with all involved. If we have to raise funds it will need all of us to agree a strategy. How about tomorrow night about 8 here?"

We all nodded agreement and then it went very quiet. The mood had changed.

So to change the subject I said mostly to Maggie "Tell you what I found a box of old family photographs before I went away and wondered if you'd like to have a look at them with me."

"Oh yes" said Maggie obviously relieved at the change of subject as I went to get the box from the dining room.

The boys were quietly chatting about sheep as Maggie and I started to sort through the box. There were pictures of the family through various stages of their lives, including Adam, Ben and Sam at various stages of their lives with their dad around the farm and some lovely ones of Maggie and Ben's wedding. Then Maggie pulled one out and after staring at it for a few minutes said "Is this your mum?" to Ben.

Ben stared at it for a minute then said "Yes but that's not dad, I think its Uncle Jonathan. It looks ……"

"Let me see" said Adam looking over his shoulder "Oh but that's a big strange."

I got up and looked over Ben's other shoulder myself shocked to see a beautiful young woman looking up adoringly into a man's face (my dad) while he had one arm around her shoulder and the other holding her hand. They were very close and looked very much a couple"

"That cant be right" I said "Did David and Jonathan look alike when they were younger. I mean you two brothers look very alike you know" I stuttered.

"Not really" said Adam "That's definitely Uncle Jonathan, not dad".

"I wonder" said Maggie very quietly "If that's the reason that Jonathan left and they never spoke again because it looks to me as though there was more than friendship between them".

None of us could stop looking at the picture. We were all equally shocked and the mood in the room had changed again dramatically.

Not long after Adam got up and brusquely said "Well I don't think we are going to solve this mystery tonight. I'll just go and check on that ewe then I think I'll get myself off to bed. Ring me Ben if you have any issues with any of the other ewes or the new lambs." And he was gone.

Maggie and Ben left shortly after and I was left alone with my thoughts and to examine the picture more closely. There was no doubt in my mind that the way the couple were looking at each other they were very much in love.

I went to bed very confused.

CHAPTER 12

That night I couldn't get to sleep with the photo on my mind and tossed and turned until the small hours. Even so I was awake early and decided the one person who I could ask about dad when he was younger was Donald. It was too early to ring him so I used the time to unpack my few bits and pieces and had some tea and toast.

As soon as I thought it was a reasonable time I rang him and he answered immediately.

"Hello Cathy are you back in Yorkshire and missing us already?" he said obviously surprised to hear from me so soon and in the early morning.

"Hi Donald, Yes I am and I hope you don't mind but I have a couple of questions for you about dad."

"Really you sound worried so I hope I can help." He said even more surprised.

"It goes back to when you first met and before he met my mum. Did he tell you the reason why he left the farm and came to live and work down South?" I decided to be direct.

He was quiet for a minute or so then answered "Yes I do Cathy he did confide in me and I suppose now he's gone its okay to tell you. He told me that he had fallen in love but the lady in question loved his brother more and she married him instead. I guess that's what you wanted to know?"

I was struggling to get my thoughts together and he went on.

"Your dad didn't feel he could stay and live around them so made the decision to come away and make a different life for himself. He met your mum a couple of years later and I'm sure you know that they were very happy together. I know that he loved your mum and you very much."

"Thank you Uncle Donald that's all I needed to know. We found a photograph of my dad and Auntie Grace which led to my questions. It actually explains a lot."

We said our goodbyes and I sat for a long time looking at the picture. It told me so much about why dad had moved away and why Uncle David had left him the house. I would have to tell the brothers what I knew as I was sure they were wondering about the photograph.

I quickly got dressed and went out the back door to Adam's house just as he was coming out of the front door.

"Can I talk to you about the photo Adam?" I said.

He hesitated for a minute then opened his front door and ushered me inside.

"I was just coming to see you although I'm not sure that I have any answers for you." he said.

As I stepped in I glanced around mostly to make sure we were alone then said "What a lovely place Adam."

It was a large open plan living room and kitchen with a log burner in one corner where Lady was curled up on a rug.

"Would you like a coffee?" he said moving towards the kitchen.

"Yes please. I think we need to talk" I needed to get it out of my system before I changed my mind.

I sat down at the breakfast bar on a stool and he quickly produced two cups of coffee from a machine in the corner.

"I really don't have any more information for you Cathy" he said rather seriously.

I told him about my phone call with Donald and what he had said and then he quietly said "Yes I thought it must be something like that just from looking at the photo but ….."

"Wait Adam there's something else." I said impatiently. "On the back of the photo is a date and I was wondering what your date of birth is?"

"I'm ahead of you Cathy because I noticed the date last night on the back of the photo. It was taken about 10 months before I was born. I wasn't going to share this today until I had time to think about it a bit more myself as the implications are obvious."

"Did your dad ever say anything to you about events before you were born" I was relieved that he realised about the date.

"No never" he mumbled this and I could see he was upset "I don't think I'll ever know now as there is nobody to tell us what went on."

"Well I've been thinking overnight and I think there is somebody who might be able to tell us" I knew I was treading on emotional ground so was taking my time.

"Who?" he looked surprised.

"Janet, the lady I met in the pub. She told me that she went to school with both our dads and also she worked for your dad after your mum died so she may be able to shed light on the situation" I said carefully.

He jumped up immediately "Janet of course! Why didn't I think of that I'll go over and see her now" getting up and picking up his mobile.

"Can I come with you please" I said hopefully.

"No! this is about me and my family" he said quite calmly..

"No Adam its about my family as well and I have a right to know" I replied angrily.

He stared at me with the phone to his ear and his look was unfathomable. Then at the other end a voice answered his call.

"Hi Janet this is Adam are you well? And Frank and the grandchildren? Yes we are all okay. Look Janet I know you might be busy but I wondered if I could call over for a chat. Well yes now would be good. There's something I need to ask you and I'm bringing my cousin Cathy with me." He glared at me as he said this.

"Come on" he said disconnecting "I suppose we might as well do this together."

It only took about 10 minutes to get to Janet's house as it was on the main road into the village.. As we entered Janet sent Frank off into the kitchen to make us all some tea and then sat down facing us in the living room.

"What do you need to ask?" she said glancing at me but looking directly at Adam.

"What do you know about my mum and Uncle Jonathan before she married my dad?" said Adam getting straight to the point.

Janet didn't look at all surprised but sighed and said "I knew one day that question might come up. Thank you." She said as Frank came in with mugs of tea on a tray putting it down and joining us.

"As you probably know we all grew up around here and went to school together. Grace and I were best friends. She was always popular she was so pretty and all the boys fancied her even my Frank" she laughed and glanced at him as he shook his head laughing "No love I only ever had eyes for you."

"Well she and Jonathan were an item from about our late teens." Janet went on. "She was crazy about him and they went everywhere together. Everybody expected them to marry especially when they got engaged on her 21st birthday."

She paused then "But a couple of months later she told me that she was pregnant. I was a bit shocked but obviously wasn't very worried as they were engaged. I said that she and Jonathan needed to come clean and tell her mum and dad then perhaps consider bringing the wedding forward as it was planned for the following year."

She paused again then took a deep breath and said "Then she told me that the baby wasn't Jonathan's and that it was David's!"

"Oh shit!" I simply couldn't help myself I was so caught up with her story but at the same time I also immediately felt a great sense of relief as I realised that Adam wasn't my dad's son. That would complicate things even more I thought.

Janet smiled at Adam lovingly "I know it was a mess at first but she really was so happy about the pregnancy. That baby was you Adam. So she went off to tell David and her parents then she had to confess to Jonathan. She didn't confide in me what his reaction was but she did tell me that they had never slept together so that she knew without any doubt it was David's baby."

I glanced at Adam. He looked relieved but didn't reply and urged her on by nodding his head.

She continued "It caused a lot of trouble obviously as Jonathan was absolutely heartbroken and he and David had an almighty row as you can imagine. Old man Thompson who was quite poorly at the time passed away a few weeks later and then Jonathan upped and left the farm soon after. I didn't see him again for many years."

"I asked Grace about him a couple of times but she just shrugged her shoulders and said it was history. She confided that she had loved Jonathan very much until she found herself gradually falling for David and he told her he had always loved her from afar. She had begun to doubt herself and realised that she and Jonathan had just got caught up with what everybody wanted and expected but that once she and David got together she knew that's who she really wanted to be with."

She went quiet then and seemed lost in her own thoughts and memories. Frank leaned across and squeezed her hand gently. She looked at him and then said "We got married about a year after them and I had my own child. Grace and I remained good friends and she had Ben then Sam. I was devastated when she died."

She continued "Then after she had gone David asked me if I knew of anyone who could help him out around the house and with the boys so I didn't hesitate. I used to take Tricia with me and they all grew up together. Tricia introduced Maggie and Ben you know."

I smiled at her and then as I turned to look at Adam I saw a mixture of emotions on his face. He got up and went over to hug Janet "Thank you so much for telling me. We found a photograph in an old box of Uncle Jonathan and mum together and it was dated about 10 months before I was born so you can imagine what went through my mind."

"Yes and I can imagine your concern but Frank was definitely your dad not Jonathan. I didn't think I would ever have to tell you or anyone else for that matter."

Then she looked at me and said "Your dad came back you know just the once for Grace's funeral and he brought you and your mum with him. I only spoke to him briefly at the wake then he was gone early the next day. I don't even know if he and Frank spoke that day. I hope this goes a little way to explaining why he left the farm and didn't come back."

"Yes it does Janet and thank you very much for letting me in on it. Now I know why I had memories of coming to the farm when I was younger." I felt quite emotional and found my eyes watering.

Shortly after that Adam and I left and on the way back to the farm we were quiet. I don't think either of us knew what to say. The whole thing had been such a revelation.

Eventually I said "Will you tell the others?"

"Yes I will as I think they have a right to know although it doesn't really affect them as much as me and you."

"Thank you for letting me come with you" I said and then as we pulled up at the house he turned to me and said "We were nearly brother and sister there so I'm glad you came to hear the story from Janet and that you now know why your dad left the farm. I'm also sorry I snapped at you it was just that I felt very confused and ….."

"Yes I now its okay" I said and leaned in and I don't know what came over me but I hugged him and gave him a peck on the cheek He looked a bit taken aback but then hugged me back.

I thought about telling him about the cousin thing at that point but immediately decided against it as I realised we had had enough emotional upset for one day. I quickly hopped out of the car and headed indoors.

CHAPTER 13

The next day I popped down to the village and did some shopping determined to be the hostess this time when we got together at the house. I wasn't a brilliant cook and settled on chilli and rice as it was something I could do with confidence.

I stopped off for a coffee and pastry again at the café and as the girl from previously was serving me a couple stopped to ask her about local accommodation. She told them to try the pub or the B&B just outside the village and as they strolled away muttering about self-catering places she came over to chat.

"Isn't there any self-catering accommodation around this area then?" I asked her.

"Well not that I know within the village area but of course there is further afield." Was her reply as she was called away to serve somebody.

An idea had begun to form in my head but I needed time to think about it so I hurried back to the house and fired up my PC jotting notes down excitedly on a pad.

Maggie came up later and helped me get to grips with he Aga and I prepared my chilli.

Everybody else arrived at the house about 8 and I served up the chilli and rice which seemed to go down quite well. Adam had obviously told them all about our chat with Janet following discovery of the photograph so the evening began more talk on the subject. For once I was able to join in and for the first time felt that I had was actually being included as part of the family.

Then talk turned to the house and my decision to sell it to them and I was surprised when it was Sam that first broached it.

"Are you absolutely sure Cathy that you want to vacate the house and sell it to us before we move forward on this."

Until that moment I didn't realise how much I didn't want to sell it so I replied slowly.

"Well since yesterday I've been thinking a bit and before I make a decision I would like your opinion – all of you."

"Perhaps I could keep the house and live in it after all and over time modernise and redecorate inside myself. Obviously I would have to get somebody in to help me as my experiences so far in life have not included decorating."

It had gone quiet with surprised eyes on me as I hesitated to say anything more but then went on.

"That's if nobody has any objections to my living here" I was beginning to feel a bit panicky. Maybe they didn't want me here after all.

Several people spoke at once but it was Adam who surprised me the most "I think that's a great idea Cathy and I for one have no objection to you staying in the house. We were just worried that you would want to let it out or sell it to strangers."

"That's something that I totally agree with you about. Since I've been here and got to know you all I've come to the realisation that it wouldn't be fair to sell it outside of the family and letting it would be even worse."

"Even though I'm pleased to hear this news I am curious why you've changed your mind so suddenly." said Ben cautiously.

"Well it was something to do with the story about my dad and Uncle David and your mum. It made me realise that I am part of this family whether you want me or not and maybe I've inherited the house for a reason. My dad walked away from everything he should have inherited and David leaving him the house was an acknowledgement of that so to let it go would be to renegade on that."

I ploughed on "I'm sorry to have been so indecisive but I myself have been through such a strange traumatic few months and …….. Its difficult to explain but when I went back to London I missed being here more than I had missed being there if you can all understand"

Maggie jumped up at this point and came over to give me the biggest hug and there were tears in her eyes when she said "Oh Cathy it would be fantastic if you stayed."

"It sounds as though you've given it quite a bit of thought" said Adam "Would you commute back to London to work or spend all your time up here?"

"No I think I would re-locate up here more or less permanently but I would need to go back from time to time as I have a family members plus friends that I would want to keep in contact with. There's also mum and dad's house to consider as it's the house I grew up in and I wouldn't want to sell it." I said thoughtfully realising that I needed to think this through carefully.

"I could set up an office in the small room at the front" I gestured towards the hallway "with a view to starting my own business."

"What sort of business?" Sam enquired.

"Similar to what I've been doing which involves sourcing properties for short term rental mostly for tourists. I could base myself here and work remotely with occasional visits out to other properties. It wouldn't entail the public coming onto your property." I said reassuringly.

Adam nodded and smiled at me thoughtfully and I felt relief rushing through my body as I realised that I had really wanted his approval.

"Well I for one think this sounds great. Perhaps you would let me help a bit with the house Cathy. It's a grand old place and I've been itching for years to modernise it." Sam said enthusiastically.

"Oh Sam I would love that and would be grateful for any ideas any of you have. I have to admit that I'm quite nervous about the whole thing. I know how busy you all are on the farm and with your own projects but any advice would be more than welcome."

"Right then." Said Sam to me "Me and you need to sit down and put our heads together. It's a bit late now but how about tomorrow morning about 9.30?" he suggested.

"Sounds good to me" I replied.

Not long after they all went there separate ways Adam and Ben again muttering about sheep and Maggie yawning loudly saying her bed was waiting for her.

I went up to bed but again struggled to sleep as I thought over all that had happened. I realised that I now felt as though these people were my family. I thought of mum and dad and wondered what they would have wanted me to do. Would they have encouraged me? I felt like I had a responsibility to mend the rift in the family.

My old life seemed like a million miles away and even though I missed Jane and Chrissie I wasn't missing Luke or even my old job.

CHAPTER 14

Next day I got a call from the estate agent to say that they had received an offer on my flat which I told them to accept. Things were beginning to come together and I just hoped I was making all the right decisions.

I had a long text from Jane telling me that she had settled in well but was going off to visit a couple more islands in the coming weeks so contact would be limited. She asked me again if I wanted to join her but I told her of my decision to stay in Yorkshire for the time being and was grateful she had thought of me.

I rang Auntie Susan to tell her my news and she didn't seem all that surprised with my decision to live in the house. "I could tell how much you had begun to enjoy the place and I'm really glad for you. Are you going to keep the house down here though?"

"Yes definitely I need a base when I come down to visit and I would find it very hard to let it go." I replied.

We chatted for some time and I said I would be coming down in a few days or so to close up the flat.

"Perhaps you and Uncle Derek could visit here when I get the house a bit more organised." I suggested.

"You know Cathy that would be really nice but it sounds like you have quite a lot of work on your hands. Anyway we'll see you in a couple of days." She replied.

Sam arrived not long after and we walked round the house chatting about what needed to be done.

"I think the first thing is to tip out anything you don't want from the bedrooms and living room" he said thoughtfully. Then we mutually agreed that the sensible thing for me to do would be to start with the small room at the front of the house and make this into an office space from where I could organise things.

"You need to speak to Adam about the broadband supplier because it might need updating if you need to set up your office in there.". He said "Will you do the decorating yourself or do you need me to put you in touch with somebody."

"You know Sam with this small room I might give it a go myself. I'm not completely useless and there's no rush but yes I think I'll need a professional to help me with the other rooms and especially the hall. Now that I've made a decision I'm itching to get going."

Sam laughed "You got for it Cathy but don't take on anything too big. I've got a mate whose a decorator so I'll give him a bell to see if he's available.

We went outside and he talked me through a few things that he thought ought to be dealt with and we agreed he should get quotes for me to get gutters cleaned and checked plus a window that needed replacing.

Over coffee later he asked "Wont you miss the buzz of city life?"

"Most definitely not. Its hard to explain but I really love the tranquillity here. After my mum and dad died I felt myself slipping into a depression but coming here and being in the beautiful countryside has really helped. I suppose because you've always lived in the country you wont understand."

"Oh yes I do I went to University in Durham and I yearned to be back here at Meadowhill and returned as often as I could. Also I had a choice with my career to set up in a city such as Leeds but I decided to try and make a go of it back here. So I do understand. I'm glad you've decided to stay."

He paused then said "You worked in the travel industry didn't you?"

"Yes, why? Are you and Katie looking to book a trip?" I laughed.

"No but I've had thoughts about setting up a business for fishing on the lake. In principal both Adam and Ben are agreeable but the stumbling block has been accommodation for people wanting to do such trips. I was thinking along the lines about self-catering accommodation" he went on.

"Well funnily enough I was talking to a girl in the village and I understand there's nothing of that type in the immediate vicinity. Were you thinking about the house or ...."

"Oh God no its far to big and not what I was thinking about at all. That's your project now for yourself." He was laughing but more seriously said "There are several empty barns at Meadowhill that would be ideal to renovate into small self-catering units. It would take a bit of work but the revenue from these could help to sustain the farm financially and I want to do my bit for the family." I could tell he was very serious and had given it some thought.

"Funnily enough its something that had crossed my mind too. My work at Dreams involved sourcing properties in rural locations, B&Bs and also self-catering accommodation so I know quite a bit on the subject." I said "But I haven't dared to mention this in front of Adam or even Ben."

"I think you'd be surprised what Ben thinks and now I've spoken to you I'm even keener. I think we should put it to them." I had to admire his enthusiasm but I was sceptical.

"Um yes. I like the way you said "we"? Do you need me to back you up?" All of a sudden I felt very anxious again.

"I was actually hoping that you would broach the subject sometime and then I could back you up" Sam said excitedly "As I say I've already spoken to Ben and he said he would be prepared to discuss some of my ideas. But Adam's a whole different subject."

"Coward" I said laughing "I'm very sceptical that Adam will listen to anything I have to say on the subject.".

"I don't agree Cathy. You'd be surprised at how highly he thinks of you and because of your experience with this sort of thing I'm sure he could be persuaded."

"Maybe" I said thoughtfully "I understand where Adam is coming from he worries about tourists traipsing all over the land and farm but it could be kept to a minimum with the right planning. Do you really think he would listen to me though? I think he still considers me to be an outsider."

"You're part of the family now. It wouldn't do any harm to give him your opinion surely." As he got up to go.

"Okay the next time we're all together I'll broach the subject" I said not really very convinced it was a good idea.

When Sam had left I immediately went back into the office and made a start by removing some of the books from the shelves and putting them into a pile on top of the desk. There were some interesting old books and I got a bit carried away looking through some of them.

Once empty I decided to try to move one of the bookshelves but it seemed to be attached to the wall in some way.

"What the hell are you doing woman? Do you want a hand?" This from Adam who appeared from nowhere.

"Well actually you've come at just the right time." I said defensively still holding onto the bookshelf which had half come away from the wall and was threatening to fall onto me.

"Here let me" as he took the weight from me and pulled it away from the wall. It had been screwed in and some plaster came away at the same time. "Don't do anymore until I find a screwdriver."

Finally between us we managed to remove the bookshelf away from the wall and he helped empty the second one of books and also pull that one away from the wall.

That'll just need refilling he said and the wallpaper needs to be removed." He said thoughtfully looking around at the very old-fashioned wallpaper.

"Yes I had already thought that" I said "I'm not frightened of getting my hands dirty" I said "I'll strip if off and ………."

He was staring at me and I realised that I must look a mess. "What oh I know I must look an absolute sight." I said nervously fingering my hair that had come down from my ponytail and was full of dust.

"Actually it suits you .. you couldn't look less like the smart city girl that arrived here a couple of months ago" He said leaning in and pulling a bit of plaster or something out of my hair as I held my breath.

"Compliments from Adam. Well that's a first" I said flustered and a bit embarrassed as I moved away from him and made myself busy picking at the edge of the wall paper to see if it would pull away easily.

"Well yes err I'm sorry if I've embarrassed you its just that you've changed so much since you first arrived and………." he looked even more embarrassed than me "Anyway I'd better get going" and muttered something about a horse.

When he'd gone I decided to go up for a shower as I realised I really was quite dirty and was shocked when I looked in the mirror to see grime streaked down my face. My head was in a whirl. I found Adam mystifying. One minute he was so pleasant and helpful and then aloof. I really did need to tell him about the cousin thing I wondered if it would make any difference about his attitude towards me. I was finding him extremely attractive and was beginning to feel that maybe he felt something too.

Why had I let this drift without telling him I thought.

That night I had yet another troubled sleep dreaming that my mum and dad had come to visit me in my new house.

CHAPTER 15

Next day I decided to take a trip to a DIY store a few miles away that Sam had suggested. I had made a list and took my time considering what I would need and came away with a supply of decorating tools and paint. I couldn't believe how much my life had changed and that my friends in London wouldn't believe the change in me. Cathy Thompson decorating her own house and living on a farm.

I arrived back with my supplies and hauled them all into the hall thinking it was a mess anyway so I may as well store things in there while I worked on the office. I decided that I would have some lunch and then make a start on stripping of the paper after.

I was in the kitchen putting a sandwich together when there was a knock on the front door. This was very unusual and I felt a bit flustered as I opened it to find Luke standing there.

"What the ……..how the hell did you find me Luke and why on earth have you come ?." I was shocked.

"Chrissie gave me the address but don't blame her I kept at her until she did." he said with a beaming smile.

I opened the door wider for him to come in "I'm not happy about this at all Luke but you've come a long way so had better come in and have a cuppa at least.".

"Are you decorating? Surely you're not planning on staying here." He looked disdainfully at all the decorating paraphernalia.

"Yes I am but that's none of your business Luke." And I gestured him through into the kitchen.

I made him a sandwich and a drink and we sat down in the kitchen on opposite sides of the table.

"Life is miserable without you Cathy and I want you to come back. I made a terrible mistake I realise that but that's finished and its you I want to be with."

I took a deep breath and said calmly "Well that's big of you Luke but I'm sorry I really don't see that there's any way back. I can never ever forgive you and it would always be there between us".

I got up moving to the sink with my empty mug and to my shock he got up and dropped down in front on me on one knee. "Cathy will you marry me?" he said holding my hand and proffering a small box in the other hand.

"Oh no for goodness sake Luke why are you doing this?" I cried in sheer panic as I knew it was the last thing I wanted or needed. "Please get up and listen to me."

He got up but didn't move away.

"Luke you really need to stop being so dramatic about this. You know as well as I do that things hadn't been right for a long time. We were just drifting along out of habit but we weren't in love, were we? You wouldn't have gone looking for somebody else if you had been in love with me."

He was quiet for a while just staring at me and then seemed to come to a sudden decision "Well I suppose part of me had decided some time ago that we things weren't right but I thought you wanted more of a commitment and if that's what you wanted then I could do that to get you to come back to me. I thought we could get engaged and then go travelling."

"Yes but it's not really what you want is it Luke?" I looked him straight back in the face. "You really want it to carry on as before meaning that you could still be the single man about town with a casual girlfriend on the side. Me having a ring on my finger won't change that will it?"

"Well yes I suppose you've got it about right" he shifted uncomfortably and moved slightly away.

"The answer is a very definite no Luke I don't want to marry you! I don't need a ring and I've decided that I'm not going travelling, well not yet anyway. I've got other plans. I've moved on and made decisions that don't include you." I said trying to smile.

I was beginning to feel a bit sorry for him as I realised he must have missed me in some way to have come all this way with a ring in his pocket.

There was a silence while he digested this then he seemed to come to a decision.

"You've changed" he said looking searchingly into my face "You've gotten hard."

"Lots has happened. First I lost mum and dad, then my job and the business with you. My life's been turned upside down in one way and another. It's made me look at things differently that's all. I don't want to drift along the way we were Luke it would just be a recipe for disaster."

He was quiet for a few minutes as though digesting things then seemed to come to a decision.

"I just thought that maybe you had been looking for more commitment from me so decided to give it one last shot but I can see you've made up your mind." He dropped my hand which he had still been holding and took a step back with a big sigh.

"Right I'd better be on my way then…..unless I can stay here overnight" he said cheekily grinning.

"Whoa I don't think that's a good idea but I could run you down into the village and book you into the pub overnight if you want. I suppose it's a long way to drive back to London in one day."

"Oh I don't know come on Cathy you know we were always good together in bed. One last night before we part" as he stepped back towards me and leaned in for a kiss. "We should end on good terms don't you think?"

"No Luke no" I said pushing him away.

There was movement from the back door oh no it was Adam "Sorry am I interrupting? If I'm not mistaken the lady said "No" he said aggressively..

He was across the room like lightening and grabbed hold of Luke by the shoulder roughly pulling him away from me.

"Hey what's your problem" as Luke turned to face him both men glaring angrily at each other.

"No Adam, its okay its not what you think." I said stepping in between them before anything further could develop.

"This is Luke my ex-boyfriend and he's just leaving, Luke this is Adam my er …. well we're related and he lives here on the farm as do the whole family." I prattled on no idea what I was saying but was very embarrassed by what had just happened. What the hell would Adam think.

The two men were still glaring angrily at each other then without moving away Adam said "Well fine but I think he needs to go now."

Luke stepped away "Its okay man I'm just off don't want to stay where I'm not welcome".

"I'm just going to take Luke down to the village to see if he can get a room. He can't drive all the way back tonight and he's not staying here." This was directed mostly at Luke.

A questioning look from Adam then "Okay pleased to meet you Luke. Sorry to have walked in like that but I heard a car and wondered who it was. Just checking Cathy was okay you know." And he backed out the way he had come in looking very uncomfortable. "You know where I am if you want me." He said nodding at me.

"Sorry Cathy I didn't mean to come on so strong" said Luke after he had gone "Looks a nice enough chap very protective and all that."

We drove down to the village and Luke booked himself a room for overnight. "Do you fancy having a drink with me tonight then?"

"No way but I'll pop down in the morning to see you off" and I turned and drove straight back to the farm feeling relieved the incident was over.

I returned as promised first thing and had a coffee with him before we hugged him said our goodbyes. He seemed resigned and almost glad to be going.

"Keep in touch" he mumbled as he drove away. "Probably not" I mumbled back.

I drove away back up to the house feeling relieved that he had gone and not at all sorry that that part of my life was finished. I needed to focus on a new beginning.

When I got back to the house a skip had arrived that Sam had promised and I spent the rest of the day stripping the old wallpaper off the office walls and then throwing it into the skip.

CHAPTER 16

Maggie rang me in the afternoon to ask how I was doing. "You've been very quiet and I understand busy making a start on the house When I get chance I'll come up and see what you've done so far."

"Yes its looking good. I've stripped most of the wallpaper off in the office now and unbelievably I'm really enjoying myself." I laughed.

"I heard about the boyfriend turning up as well would love to hear more. When you're free give me a call and come down."

"There are loads of books here Maggie that I thought might be useful for the boys so wondered what you thought before I consider getting rid of them."

"It's so very busy at the moment and I don't seem to have time for anything." said Maggie apologetically "We lost a ewe during birthing last night and so have two orphaned lambs that need to be reared. Please hang on to the books for me as they sound great for the boys. Do you fancy coming down here later for something to eat and they can show you the lambs?"

So later I wondered down before the boy's bedtime to see the lambs and piglets. They were so cute and it was wonderful to watch the boys feeding them in the kitchen of the cottage. "Do you keep them in here?" I enquired noticing a few old towels on the floor at the side of the Aga.

"Well we could probably keep them in the barn but Ben thinks its good for the boys to help rear them and its more convenient for me if they're here. Gives them a bit of responsibility and teaches them about animal life." She laughed "I draw a line at having the piglets living in the house though."

We went out to inspect the piglets and then Ben arrived not long after looking exhausted and we all sat down to eat together. Maggie took the boys up for a bath and I stayed to chat as I was genuinely interested to hear about all that had been happening on the farm.

When Maggie rejoined us she started to tell me about a birthday party she was organising for the twins. It was to be at the farm and they had invited several of their school friends.

"It sounds lovely" I said "Especially the bouncy castle. Am I invited? Id love to come."

"Of course" said Maggie enthusiastically "In fact I was hoping you would be able to help. You are part of the family now so it's a given that you have to get involved."

I laughed then she went on "Tell me more about the incident with the ex. Adam said he was being a bit pushy with you and he got a bit worried".

"Yes well unfortunately he came in at just the wrong moment and got the wrong end of the stick. Luke just tried to kiss me that's all but Adam was very gallant even though I had it under control."

So I told her all about him proposing and me telling him emphatically that we were finished and when I was done she just nodded but glanced over at Ben with a strange look on her face.

"What?" the look puzzled me.

"Nothing" she said "We're just so pleased to have you here."

"Oh okay" I said relieved that it was nothing more.

"Actually while I've got you both here there were some other ideas that Sam and I were discussing and I wondered what your reaction would be"

"Go on try us" said Maggie.

"Sam and I were talking about his ideas re fishing parties and he said that he had discussed this with you Ben" I ventured.

"Yes" said Ben "I think it's a great idea but he was talking about accommodation here on the land and I'm not so sure about that."

"No" I said cautiously "He thinks that one or two of the derelict barns could be renovated into self-catering units which I also think is a very good idea. With my experience he thought I might be able to help."

"Well" said Ben thoughtfully "I myself think its something worth looking into but I'm not sure where Adam would be on this."

"Yes I know that's what Sam and I discussed" I replied hesitantly.

Ben and Maggie looked at each other and both started laughing "So he thought you could broach it with us first."

"Actually yes he's asked me to bring it up the next time we're all together. It was a spur of the minute thing that I've just told you about it now but I suppose I was looking at getting your backing first and I see now that's what Ben has done with me." I said joining in the laughing.

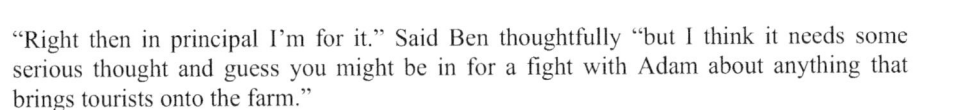

"Right then in principal I'm for it." Said Ben thoughtfully "but I think it needs some serious thought and guess you might be in for a fight with Adam about anything that brings tourists onto the farm."

"I think we also have to be careful not to let him think that we are ganging up on him" said Maggie "My feeling is that Adam feels as the older brother he has a responsibility to make sure the farm, lake and all the land is protected. He takes it very serious, maybe a bit too serious at times."

"Yes Maggie's right." Said Ben smiling at his wife "By all means broach it next time we're altogether Cathy and we'll see what happens."

"I'm off back to London tomorrow as I've sold my flat and have to move the rest of my stuff. I'll only be gone a couple of days and will be back to help organise the party. Maybe that would be a good day to broach it." I said happy that we had at least discussed it.

CHAPTER 17

It was strange the next day stepping back inside my cold and unlived in flat so I didn't take long sorting out the possessions I had left behind. I phoned a removal company and arranged for my bed and bedroom furniture, my couch and TV to be transported up to Yorkshire later in the week along with some of the other bulkier items. I had done a deal with the buyer re the white goods so gave the fridge and cooker a thorough clean then leaving my beloved coffee machine and other smaller items in the hallway to collect to transport myself on my return journey back to Yorkshire I drove over to mum and dad's house.

Over the next two days I cleared out even more of mum and dad's old possessions, including clothes, shoes and household ornaments keeping to one side things I wished to take back with me and leaving a minimum in the house. I decided that if I was to keep the house to return to from time to time then I would prefer to keep it as uncluttered as possible.

Chrissie invited me to her house for a meal with her and Rob. Her pregnancy was advancing now and she was absolutely glowing with happiness. Rob had decorated the baby's bedroom in a beautiful muted yellow with Beatrix Potter figures stencilled on one wall. It was absolutely gorgeous and I felt so honoured to be able to share in their happiness. Much to Chrissie's amusement Rob and I got into quite an intensive discussion about our growing mutual decorating techniques.

I also called on Auntie Susan who was also busy planning for a new arrival as her daughter was due to give birth to a second grandchild in a month or so.

"You seem so much happier Cathy now that you have made such huge decisions in your life. Is there a man involved in all this" she laughed with a twinkle in her eye.

"Oh no Auntie Susan nothing of the sort. I won't be looking for a new man in my life for a long time now that the Luke episode is finished and I have enough work and plans on the house to me out of mischief for the foreseeable ." I laughed back with her.

"I'm just glad that he has gone because I didn't like him much and neither did your mum" she surprised me with this.

"Mum never said a word". I said raising my eyebrows.

"No well she wouldn't have wanted to interfere but I know she thought he wasn't the settling down kind of fella and I felt he was too full of himself and his own interests."

I nodded as I thought about this and realised how true that was.

"Well you'll be the first to know if there's a new man comes into my life but I wouldn't hold your breath." I reassured her.

A couple of days later I loaded up the car with as much as I could, collected the stuff from the flat, dropped my keys off at the estate agent then journeyed back up the M6 at a leisurely pace. I felt more in control of my life than I had done for a long time.

As I drove the last few miles I felt a wonderful sensation of coming home, the sight of hedgerows with a splash of colour from the many dandelions and other spring flowers gave me a feeling of continuity and hope. I had not had feelings like this since before losing my parents and I realised I was slowly beginning to heal then immediately felt guilty which I knew was silly but I still missed them so very much.

The rest of the week I spent continuing my work in the office. Sam had kindly arranged for a friend of his called Steve, a decorator to come and paint the ceiling and as I had decided against wallpaper I was now ready to start painting the walls. I was no decorator and knew my limitations so had asked Steve if he could come back and do all the woodwork for me. He also said he could paint the bookshelves as this would smarten them up.

When my furniture arrived from London I asked the removal men to put it all in one of the garages as I had decided to store it for the time being until I was a bit more organised.

I felt as though I was inching my way to making the house my own.

Saturday dawned bright and dry so about mid-morning I sauntered down to the farm to make a start on the party food with Maggie and Carole. By lunchtime all the food was prepared, a table had been set up outside the back door for the eight invited children and a couple of lads set up the bouncy castle. Katie arrived to help but Ben and Sam were busy on the farm and Adam was apparently busy at his surgery.

A lovely couple of hours was spent watching the children throwing themselves around with wild abandonment on the bouncy castle and running around generally getting very hot and bothered. Maggie then quietened them all down a bit and got them to sit and eat their food following which Paul took them off with Carole to show off some of the animals to the visiting children.

As the afternoon wore on parents began to arrive to take the children home and after opening a couple of bottles of wine Maggie and her mum produced more food so we all sat down outside to relax after the busy day. The boys were allowed back on the bouncy castle for a while and Ben, Adam and Sam eventually joined us.

As I took a sip of wine Carole asked me about my progress at the house.

"Well I've made a start in the room at the front as I intend it to be my office. Its actually almost finished." I said with pride. "You'll have to walk up and see what's been done so far. What about a girl's night with just you, Maggie, Katie and me." I suggested.

"I'd like that very much." Said Carole nodding enthusiastically.

"Sounds great" from Katie "Do you intend to start with your little business venture soon?"

"Yes, once the rooms finished and I can get the IT sorted out" I replied with a nod at Adam who had been sorting this out for me "I'm also going to move forward with renovating the house. I'm employing Steve, a friend of Sam's, to help me with some of the decorating and we are looking to work in the living room next."

I saw out of the corner of my eye Sam looking at me and realised that he thought this would be a good time to start our talks so I took a deep breath and continued.

"Talking about moving forward I've been having some other ideas. Sam had mentioned that he would like to start up fishing parties on one area of the lake and I had wondered if anybody had thought about self-catering units here on the farm."

There was a palpable pause then

"No! No!" burst out Adam slightly rising in his chair "That's exactly what we don't want".

"Now hold on there Adam. Let her have her say." This was from Ben who patiently put his hand on his brother's arm.

"Go on Cathy" Maggie encouraged.

"Well there are two old barns behind the big house that could definitely be renovated for such use."

"That's a hell of a lot of work" said Ben not looking at Adam "And would we need to employ staff. Would it be worth the financial outlay do you think?"

At this point I paused as I ran out of courage and it was Sam that interceded.

"This is very interesting as its similar to what I had suggested last year when I mentioned setting up fishing groups. I think Cathy's got something here and that we should talk about it a bit more." He smiled over at me but glanced towards Adam to gauge his reaction.

"Yes I realise that it would be a lot of work but I would be happy to manage it and come on board financially if that would help. I have sold my flat and also inherited quite a bit of money so surely with Sam's contacts it would be worth discussing at least."

By this time I swear I could see steam coming out of Adam's ears he looked so angry as he shook his head from side to side.

He got up angrily his chair falling back on the floor making Lady jump up in surprise as she was sat behind him. "I'm not prepared to discuss this anymore. ………. No! Emphatically No!!". He glared at me and the room in general then stormed out.

Maggie's hand was on my arm as I got up to follow "No leave him. Let him digest it."

Katie started giggling and we all turned to look at her "Sorry but I've never seen Adam like that. He always seems such a gentleman and very controlled and ……. It just made me laugh" she mumbled going quite pink.

Sam put his arm round her and then also laughing said "It certainly ruffled his feathers."

"Well" said Ben deciding to take charge "I think that Sam and I need to have a long talk with Adam. What do you say Maggie? You've been very quiet through all this."

"Loosely I think some of Cathy and Sam's ideas are good but I cant see you or dad becoming too involved as you have enough to do running the farm and Adam is busy with his practice. If Cathy is prepared to come on board permanently and help develop these ideas then I would be very happy. I am just thrilled that she is staying here." And she put her arm round me squeezing tight.

Adam came back in then "Sorry guys what with the recent revelations and …………..its been a bit ………. Anyway I shouldn't have gone off like a child but I'm still not up for this."

Then he turned to me "With all due respect Cathy what the hell do you know about this place and how it is run. You have no idea about the struggles to keep it afloat. It's a 24/7 thing each of us doing our own individual jobs. Its all very well talking about making a couple of out-buildings into pretty little holiday lets but it would take a lot of money and work and I cant see it being worth it. On top of that you know that we don't want all and sundry wondering about the farm."

The atmosphere was very stiff as we said goodnight but Adam turned to me and said "If you want a lift up to the house my car's outside?"

"Yes that would be great" I said a bit relieved as Carole had given me some of the left over food and I was worried about carrying it.

We drove up to the house in silence and then as we pulled up outside he said "Look don't take this too personal you're part of the family now and therefore you have a right to give your opinion but on this one we have to agree to disagree if that's okay with you".

That was it. The moment that I made the decision as I decided that I had nothing to lose and needed to tell him.

"Adam I need to tell you something else. Its been on my mind for ages." I said turning in my seat to look directly at him.

"What?" he was actually smiling at me which unnerved me slightly as I continued anyway. This had gone on for far too long.

"I'm not your cousin" I didn't mean to be so blunt but as usual my mouth took over.

The smile had gone and he looked aghast. "What? What do you mean? Who the hell are you then? Have you been lying about who you are all this time? Are you an imposter? I knew there was something fishy and you were after something right from the start."

"For God's sake Adam calm down. Of course I'm not an imposter! Do you think Mr Knowles would have given me the house and sent me here if he wasn't sure about who I was." I was shocked and exasperated with his reaction and felt my anger rising with the injustice of his insinuations.

"Do you know what Adam I've had enough of you and your angry outbursts. I'm going into MY house and when you've calmed down tomorrow we'll talk some more" I jumped out of the car spilling sausage rolls onto the ground as I headed straight for the front door. I was angrier than I had been in a long time.

This man was ridiculous. He was able to switch from nice to nasty in seconds and this always seemed to be aimed at me. What the hell had I done for him to have taken such a dislike to me from day one. I felt quite indignant at his suggestions that I was an imposter and out for what I could get.

CHAPTER 17

I didn't sleep at all that night and thought about going to see Adam first but decided to leave it to give myself time to calm down. I was shocked at his reaction to my finally telling him about not actually being his cousin. Perhaps when he had time to think things through he would be more willing to let me explain properly.

Steve arrived to paint the bookshelves so as there wasn't room for us both to work in the office at the same time I took myself off for a bit of fresh air. As I walked through the garden and then down the pasture towards the lake I breathed in the fresh air then turned around to look back at the house. It looked so beautiful in the sunshine and I felt a great deal of regret that my dad had decided to leave but realised that if he had stayed then he wouldn't have met my mum and I wouldn't have been here at all.

The more I thought about it as I stood there looking back at the house I realised that I wanted to stay. It didn't matter about the ideas Sam and I had about the self-catering units. If Adam wasn't interested and it was decided not to progress then so be it. I didn't want to be around him anymore than he obviously didn't want to be around me.

Returning to the house I found Steve just packing up for the day having made a beautiful job of the bookshelves. I couldn't do any more until they were fully dry so I locked up the house deciding to pop down to the village for some groceries.

On my way back I parked up at the farm thinking I should tell Maggie and anybody else that was around about the cousin thing before Adam told them first.

As I entered the open front door I could hear voices and realised it was Adam shouting

"She's a spoilt city bitch with no idea what this place means to us all I for one am sick of the whole sorry mess and her interference. Not only has she got the family property by deception but also wants to turn the place into a holiday complex. On top of that she's setting us all against each other which we've never done before. I wish she had never come here."

I turned to see Carole with the boys behind me and shock on her face

"Have you come to see the lambs again Cathy?" says one of the boys.

"No sorry not today" I muttered on a sob and ran out of the house back to my car.

"Cathy wait" called Carole but by that time I was in the car.

As I parked up at the front of the house I realised I was shaking and wasn't sure if this was with anger or shock. I sat there for a minute or two trying to reign in the sobs then instead of going in decided to go for another walk to calm myself down. I blindly walked round the side of the house towards the back and down the garden towards the lake retracing my steps from earlier desperately needing to be alone.

I was devastated after hearing what Adam thought of me. Was I a spoilt bitch with only my own interests in mind? I wasn't an imposter! The house was legally mine but I obviously didn't fit in here and Adam in particular didn't want me here so the best thing I could do would be to pack up and walk away.

There was no way I could stay here under these awful circumstances so I would just leave and give them the house. It belonged to the family – a family I wasn't a part of.

The overwhelming feeling of sadness and devastation Id had when mum and dad died returned with a vengeance. Well never mind I thought at least I still had mum and dad's house I would just have to go back and pick up from there. But why did I feel so horribly miserable at this idea.

CHAPTER 18

By this time without even realising where I was going I had reached the lake and sat down on a large rock just gazing out over the water watching the birds swoop down occasionally It was so tranquil here it calmed my mind.

Looking towards the water I could see something red just near the shore and went forward to investigate. The rocks were slippery from the downpour we'd had earlier so I stepped carefully but just then my foot slipped and I felt myself losing balance. I landed on my backside none too gently and immediately tried to get up but found my foot had wedged down between the rocks. I sat back and laughed and laughed at myself. Adam was right I didn't belong here. I couldn't even go for a walk without getting myself into a pickle.

After trying for about 10 minutes I couldn't free my foot so I started to try to undo the laces on my trainers and take my foot out but it was too tightly wedged and I couldn't get far enough down to undo them. I began to get a bit worried and finding that I simply couldn't get my foot out no matter how much I twisted and pulled which actually hurt now.

I reluctantly decided I needed to call for help and reached in my pocket for my phone. Damn damn it wasn't there and I remembered I had it in my hand as I walked down to the shore and there it was a few feet away lying between two rocks. There was no way I could reach it from my awkward position. I frantically looked around for a stick or something to reach for it but there was nothing. Absolutely nothing and the more I struggled the more painful my ankle was getting.

Now I was beginning to panic as I realised that nobody knew where I was and who would think to look here even if they cared enough. Maggie and everybody at the farm would think Id gone to bed and wouldn't check on me maybe for a day or so. It had started to drizzle and I was becoming wet and cold and frightened. My phone rang several times but all I could do was watch it from a distance as it lit up.

As time went on the light began to fade and I began to lose hope and thought perhaps I was going to die here. Accepting that nobody was coming I tried to lay down with my head on a smooth rock and even though it was very uncomfortable I was beginning to feel very tired.

I had no idea of the time or how long I had been here until I became aware of an animal panting close by and froze in absolute terror. I had no defence and thought was it a fox or something else. Did foxes attack and bite people? I didn't know but felt complete and utter fear. It seemed to be getting closer and then it was right next to me and it was going to attack me.

The panting was next to my ear now and then a cold nose touched my cheek and a dog barked loudly. I screamed in terror and then with relief through the darkness as I saw the outline of a man's figure walking towards me over the rocks.

"What the hell are you doing here? Are you hurt? Thank God. We've been worried sick." It was Adam. "Its okay good girl you found her".

I realised gratefully that it was Lucy his dog that had found me prodding me with her cold nose.

"What the hell Cathy? Why are you down here? Can you move?"

"No my foot is stuck and I couldn't reach my phone" I was crying and I must have sounded hysterical as I tried to explain.

I felt him gently ease a couple of the larger rocks to one side and release my foot. I winced with the pain as he did so. He very gently felt it "I don't think its broken it might be just a sprain."

"I'm so sorry" I mumbled I felt sick and dizzy.

"Look you're obvious in shock and there's no way you can walk so here hook your arm around my neck and I'll carry you." He scooped me up like I was a feather. His body was warm and strong and he smelt beautiful of something musky. He was very quiet as he made his way back up the embankment concentrating on getting me away from the lake. Next we were at his car and placed me in the back and threw a blanket over me just as another jeep pulled up next to his.

It was Ben "My God where was she? Is she hurt? "

Adam quickly explained and said "We need to get her somewhere warm and comfortable. My place is nearest and I can check her ankle there plus any medication. Can you go back up to the farm and let everybody know that she's okay and I'll ring you in a bit."

It wasn't long before I was carried by strong arms into his house and laid gently down on the couch. My ankle was throbbing and I was soaking wet.

"We need to get you out of these wet clothes" as he helped me out of my coat.

He disappeared for a minute then came back with a big towelling dressing gown and with his help I managed to pull my jumper up over my head whilst he pulled my jeans down and wrapped the dressing gown around me.

At any other time I would have been embarrassed by him seeing me in my knickers and bra but I couldn't have cared less. I felt so sleepy and couldn't stop sobbing during the whole ordeal. After settling me back on the sofa with pillows and throwing a fleece blanket over me he then gently examined my ankle properly and said "It's not broken but badly sprained and bruised so I'm going to bandage it for support."

He was very gentle and once done he disappeared for a couple of minutes again and came back with a mug of warm tea. "Here drink this and take these tablets they'll take the edge of the pain" as he helped me lift the cup and I sipped the warm liquid.

"You're in shock but this should help" I could feel the hot drink warming inside me and as his face came into focus I could see the concern on his face.

"I feel so sleepy. I'm so sorry." I muttered as I could feel my eyelids getting heavy.

"That's it just sleep" was the last thing I heard.

I woke a few hours later to see Lucy on the floor next to me and Adam stretched out in an armchair opposite. As I took in my surroundings I realised I must have been there for some time as it was light outside. As I stirred realising I needed the loo he woke with a start. "Are you okay? Are you still in pain?" he sounded concerned. "No I said I just need the toilet"

"Take it slowly and lean on me " he said as he helped me slowly into the bathroom and then exited to give me privacy but came back in and half carried me back to the couch just as Maggie appeared " Thank goodness you're okay" she said "When you didn't answer your phone and there was no sign of you anywhere we got worried. Your car was still there with your groceries in so we knew you hadn't gone far".

"It was damned irresponsible" blurted Adam angrily "What the hell were you doing down there? We thought that boyfriend of yours had carried you off somewhere. Why did you have trainers on I thought you'd bought proper walking boots."

"I………I" and to my shame I burst out crying again.

"Adam stop she's upset and had a terrible shock. Lets get you back to the house and maybe up to your own bed" said Maggie. " Or I could put clean bedding on the bed in the living room for the time being if you cant get upstairs."

"No" said Adam looking a bit sheepish at his outburst "She must stay here where I can keep an eye on her. There's no way she can get upstairs to her room and she's definitely not sleeping in the bed that dad died in. I'll work from home today there's loads of paperwork to catch up on."

"Please I need to go I'm so sorry to have caused such upset but I can manage" as I desperately tried to get up but swayed as I did so.

"No lie back down where you are" said Adam gently this time pushing me back onto the couch.

I didn't really have much choice and they settled me back on the couch with Maggie fussing over me bringing another hot drink and some toast. Adam had another look at my ankle and decided it definitely was only sprained so re-bandaged it and gave me some more tablets.

For the rest of the day I dozed on Adams very comfortable couch. Lucy never left my side and I stroked her gently from time to time letting her know how grateful I was.

Adam had disappeared and Maggie had returned to check on me. "How are you feeling now?" she said still looking concerned.

"A lot better thank you but I'm so sorry to have worried everybody so much. You must have a million things to do instead of being here checking on me. I'm going to get myself up and once I'm fully recovered I plan to move back to London and sell the house." I said feeling very determined but the tears were again falling down my face. I felt so bereft and empty.

"Oh for goodness sake Cathy none of us wants that. You've got it all wrong." She said with a big sigh sitting down on the sofa next to me.

"I don't know what on earth has gone on with you two and I'm not sure which one of you I feel more sorry for I've never seen Adam in such a state and look at you."

"Oh Maggie I've made such a mess of things and I need to tell somebody the truth." So between sobs I explained about my dad bringing me up as his even though he wasn't my birth father. Mum was pregnant when she met him by some random guy who left her when she told him she was expecting. She fell in love with my dad and they married soon after. They were very happy together and he was the only dad I ever knew."

"He legally adopted me when I was one year old and after they died the solicitor explained that I was legally entitled to the house etc. I should have explained all this at the beginning and I did try to once or twice but didn't and then Adam thought I was his sister and then…!" I trailed off on a gulp and looked up at Maggie to see her with the biggest smile on her face I had seen since I arrived at Meadowhill.

"What a wonderful story Cathy but you see I've known for some time that you and Adam were attracted to each other. I don't think the cousin thing is important although it might have caused problems if you'd been his sister" This made me laugh but she carried on.

"Do you not realise that Adam is crazy about you that's why he's so angry all the time?" she looked questioningly at me.

This made me cry even more. "No I think you must be wrong Maggie. He thinks I'm some sort of imposter………." But then I saw her eyes shift to look behind me.

There he was filling the doorway with a big beaming smile on his face.

"Oh uh I'm off I'll leave you two to sort things out. I really have got better things to do on the farm." said Maggie disappearing quickly through the doorway as he moved forward.

"How much of that did you hear." I said nervously.

"All of it. Look lets start again." He said as he pulled the armchair to sit opposite me. He gulped then said.

"Firstly I apologise for what you overheard. Carole told us that you had run out but you'd gone before I could go after you. I really am so ashamed and need to tell you that actually you're the best thing that's happened to Meadowhill in a long while." His smile faded as he splayed his hands almost appealing for me to understand "And to me for that matter." He added for good measure.

"I'm so sorry to have doubted you and said those awful things it wouldn't have mattered even if you had been my cousin. I think I fell in love with you the first time I saw you."

I hadn't spoken but then I reached forward and pulled him towards me and his arms were round me in an instant and then we were kissing and it felt so wonderful. I was home this was were I was meant to be I thought as he stopped and tilted my chin up to look into my face very intently.

"Are you upset that he's gone?" he said anxiously..

"Who? Luke? Definitely not I didn't invite him he just turned up when my friend gave in to him and told him where I was. Lets forget Luke, forget Stella This is just about you and me and……….."

He stopped me with another kiss then came up for air and said "I've been such a fool".

"I think we both have but just kiss me like that again." I smiled up at him and he did again and again.

CHAPTER 19

A few days later I was well enough to return to the house and with Adam's help hobbled up the stairs. I felt much better in myself but my ankle was still a bit painful and was horribly bruised.

"You could have stayed for longer." Said Adam that evening as we were sat having a glass of wine.

"Yes your house is very comfortable but I like this house and feel attached to it. Its my home now. You could always move in here." I said seductively.

"Oh Cathy Thompson I'm shocked. You have become so forward." He laughed. "Actually I know its early days but I was thinking much the same."

"Listen I need to tell you something" he said on a more serious note.

"Ben and Sam have been talking to me about what we all argued about regarding your ideas. I tentatively agree and think we should discuss it more fully." He seemed quite keen now that he had had time to digest the idea.

"I wouldn't want you to agree just because of me" I said cautiously and kissed him "Lets have one of our get togethers as a family and discuss it more fully and see how we go from there. Now about you moving in." I said as he pulled me to my feet and said "In that case I think I should explore your bedroom and in particular your bed to see if I think it's up to my standard."

Three months later…………..

It was the end of August and a beautiful hot sunny day. We were all sat outside the house having an evening meal with a table set up on the lawn. It had been a busy week or so on the farm with haymaking in full swing but we had decided that we all needed a break and so this evening had been decided on. As we had opted for an outside meal Sam and Adam were barbequing sausages, chicken and steaks to go with the salad and potatoes I had prepared.

Adam had moved into the house with me a month earlier. I hadn't as yet set up my business as I had been far too busy renovating and decorating the house. The office was up and running and the living room had been completely cleaned out and stripped back ready to be redecorated. We were certainly keeping Steve busy as he was also set to decorate a couple of the bedrooms and Adam had got a firm in to give quotes for new plumbing in the main bathroom.

It really was beginning to feel like home especially as I had moved in some of my furniture and bits and pieces from mum and dad's house along with the things we had kept of the family's.

As regards the development of the self-catering units Sam had drawn up some plans and we were awaiting planning permission before starting work on them. Adam had suggested that we also use his barn for letting now that he had vacated it and as this property was more or less ready market once the other units were up and running we would be ready to advertise.

I was to manage the properties and together with Sam's fishing business book people into them. We had interviewed a couple of girls from the village to help with housekeeping and so slowly it was all coming together.

What was even more important was that it was amicable and in fact once Adam had got over his earlier misgivings he had got involved with all aspects of the project. He had a gate erected between the house and the units and barn conversation so that anybody who was booked in wouldn't need to access the farm or its properties as they could come and go via the lane from the main road and the dirt track down to the lake through the trees.

"Penny for your thoughts" said Maggie in my ear.

"Sorry I was just thinking how happy I am and how much I'm enjoying belonging here. It's as though it was meant to be all along." I said happily.

I was watching the boys run around kicking a ball on the lawn and thinking of my dad and Uncle David doing the same thing all those years ago, and then Adam, Ben and Sam as they were growing up.

"I know its sad that Uncle David and my dad fell out for most of their lives but if they hadn't then we all probably wouldn't be here today so I feel content that this would have made them happy" I said spreading my hands to include us all.

"You must still miss your mum and dad" Maggie sympathised. We had grown closer over the last few months and relied on each other enormously. I liked to think that she felt the same as me and that we were like the sisters that neither of us ever had.

"Yes but it has got easier in the last month or so although I am looking forward to Auntie Susan visiting next week." I said laughing as the ball bounced over my head and into the flower bed behind.

"Careful boys Cathy could get hurt" she said looking a bit concerned.

"For goodness sake don't be silly Maggie they're having such fun" I leaned towards her as she whispered "Did you take the test?"

"Yes" I smiled a secret smile "I'll tell him tonight". Her arms were around me instantly hugging me tight.

I was so lost in my thoughts that I hadn't noticed it go quiet until I turned my head to see Adam approach and get down on one knee in front of me.

"Cathy Thompson I love you." he said looking lovingly into my eyes "Will you marry me?"

I paused for a couple of heartbeats savouring the moment then seeing a questioning look in his eyes I quickly replied "Yes I'll marry you Adam Thompson" and as he slipped the ring on my finger I leaned in for a kiss and whispered my news.

His face lit up with happiness and then as everybody realised what was happening there was a cacophony of noise with everybody hugging and kissing their congratulations. Even the boys ran over to join in

The family rift was finally complete and life at Meadowhill would continue with the Thompson family in residence.

.

Printed in Great Britain
by Amazon